CW00865732

A Surprise for Christine

A Surprise for Christine

And other lighthearted short stories

Eileen Thornton

All the short stories included in this anthology have been previously
published in national magazines in the United Kingdom.

Contents

A Surprise for Christine

I had never seen my friend Christine looking so low. She was normally such a cheerful person, always bouncing back no matter what the trouble. But I had to admit, being made redundant at twenty-seven was pretty depressing on its own without having her boyfriend leave her for some brassy blonde.

Making my way to meet Jean and a few other friends, I wondered if there was anything I could do to put the smile back on her face. Normally she joined us at these Monday evening get-togethers, but tonight she had promised to help her mother with some dressmaking.

Naturally the others were sorry to learn that Christine's boyfriend had left her.

"Isn't that just like a man to kick you when you're down?" said Jean.

I agreed, adding it would be nice if we could do something to cheer her up. "Does anyone have any suggestions?"

The girls sipped at their drinks, while giving the matter some thought.

"What about a party?" said Ann at last.

"I don't know; is she really in the mood for…?" Jean began.

But I quickly interrupted. "Hang on, that's a good idea. It's Christine's birthday next Saturday, why don't we give her a surprise party?"

"Well, if you're sure. I just wonder if she'll want so much fuss at the moment." Jean sounded doubtful.

"Of course she will," I replied. "Fuss is exactly what she needs. Throwing this party will show how much we all care. But we only have until Saturday so we need to set out a plan of action."

By the end of the evening it was agreed that we would hold the party in the community hall. Being on the village green and close to the duck pond made it the ideal setting for a summer party.

We had also made a guest list. Ann, having recently completed a course in computers, offered to print the invitations. We decided that the party should start at 7pm prompt; therefore it was important that all the guests were in the hall by 6.30pm at the latest. Any one arriving after that would stand a chance of bumping into Christine and the whole surprise would be spoilt.

My head buzzed as I walked home. For some reason I had yet to fathom, I'd volunteered to make the cake. I must have had too much wine. My skill at cake making went no further than fairy cakes.

Vi had promised she would decorate it on Friday, which meant I had to make the wretched thing tomorrow; allowing it a few days to settle down. Now, what else had I said I would do? Oh yes. I was going to ask my brother to provide the music.

Suddenly I panicked. It had been very rash of me to offer Jerry's services. He is into heavy beat; what we really wanted was something light for a summer evening.

But he had just set up a band and I knew he would relish the opportunity to play to a live audience, even if it was for nothing. Nevertheless, I would need to make it clear exactly what we wanted.

We all met up again the following evening having decided to get together every day until the party.

"I've made the cake." I gave Vi a sheepish grin. "I'm afraid it's sunk a little. Well, quite a lot actually; I'm hoping you can do a repair job with the icing." I hastily went on to say I had explained to Jerry what we wanted and he was more than happy to provide the music.

I crossed my fingers under the table. He had appeared to take in what I said, but I couldn't really be sure. Jerry was always inclined to do his own thing.

Ann told us she had booked the hall for the whole day, giving us time to decorate it. She had also brought a copy of the invitation cards for approval, saying she would post them the following day if everyone was happy.

Some of the others had already started making cakes, sausage rolls and quiches to freeze. Sandwiches and other such items would be made on the day. So far everything was going to plan.

By Friday all Christine's friends had telephoned to accept the invitation to the party, promising faithfully to be there before 6.30. Everyone who knew of the surprise had been sworn to secrecy. I had kept well away from Christine, fearing I may slip up and give the game away.

I was picking up the fresh bread and rolls the next morning, while wine, nuts and crisps were already stored in Ann's garage. Everything was organized; nothing could go wrong. We would simply set up the hall in the morning and then lock the door until we needed to lay out the food.

I awoke to a lovely sunny morning. Normally on a Saturday I enjoyed a lie in, but today there wasn't a moment to lose.

The hall was buzzing with activity when I burst through the door. Ann was in the middle of blowing up a balloon. Startled at my sudden entrance, it slipped through her fingers and whizzed around the hall, making everyone laugh.

"I don't think I can blow up many more of these," said Ann, when the laughter had subsided. "It's more difficult than I thought; I haven't enough puff."

"Don't worry, we'll all take a turn," I assured her. Though I wasn't sure how we would manage it if Ann couldn't. Being a superb diver, her lungs were far superior to ours.

Meanwhile, Helen was making a good job of the floral arrangement, which would be the centre-piece on the table and Ann's rather pompous brother, David was up a ladder. He had volunteered to fasten a large net onto the ceiling. It would hold the blown-up balloons. At the appointed time, a single thread would be pulled allowing them all to fall on the guests below.

"There, what do you think of that? I bet you girls couldn't have made such a good job of it." David made a gesture towards the net only to lose his footing on the ladder.

His hands, thrashing around at the empty air, caught hold of a cord, which turned out to be the switch for the three large newly-installed ceiling fans. The sudden yank on the cord caused the three fans to spring into action at high speed, blowing Helen's delicate blooms off the table.

"Turn it off!" she yelled, clutching her precious flowers to her ample bosom. "You idiot! What are you playing at?"

"I'm sorry," said David, still wobbling perilously on the ladder; one hand frantically grabbing out for something more stable. Unfortunately, he caught hold of the balloon net and, being only fastened with a four small pins, it came away causing him to crash to the floor. Ann and I rushed over to where he was desperately trying to disentangle himself from the net. We burst out laughing at the scene.

Once he had managed to free himself, David jumped to his feet, red-faced with embarrassment. He threw the net to the ground. "If you can do any better, then you'd best get on with it."

"I'm sorry," I said, stifling my laughter. "We shouldn't laugh. Are you alright?"

He nodded his face still very red.

"You're making such a good job of it, David, we'd be most grateful if you'd put it up again." A sudden thought struck me. "And after that, would you be an angel and blow up the balloons. I really appreciate you offering to help us; I know we couldn't manage without you." I gave the girls a sly grin.

"Well, I suppose if you put it like that I could stay a while longer," said David, recovering his dignity. "How many balloons are there?"

"Thank you David. There's quite a lot actually, but you needn't blow up them all, a couple of hundred or so will do."

He looked horrified. Giving him my most endearing smile, I moved swiftly across to the kitchen where Jean and Mary were standing ready to make the sandwiches.

"What happened out there?" Mary nodded towards the hall.

"David was fooling around with the ladder." I grinned, recalling the scene.

"Didn't you tell him we don't have time to fool around?" said Jean.

"Yes, you're right," I said. "I have the bread in the car; perhaps you could give me a hand to bring it in."

Jean and Mary gaped at me. "We've brought the bread," said Mary at last. "We thought you were bringing some of the fillings."

I was stunned. "No it was the other way around. See, it's written here." I pulled my list from my pocket.

"No. Bread is definitely on our list," said Jean, pulling it from her bag. "Mary and I were to collect and pay for the bread. Let me see." She paused, running her finger down the page. "There!" she said triumphantly. "Order and collect loaves. It says you and Helen were to buy the fillings between you."

I closed my eyes and took a deep breath. "Well," I said at last. "This is a fine state of affairs. We're going to have to do some quick thinking. I only hope no one else brings bread." I called Helen and Ann into the kitchen and began to explain the problem.

"Really! Women! Can't you do anything right?" David's head appeared around the door.

I reminded him of his recent tussle with the balloon net and what his friends might make of it if they were to hear. He slunk away without another word.

"Helen, have you brought anything we can use for sandwiches?" I asked, getting straight to the point.

"Yes. Bread and rolls, they're in my car." She looked at the expression on our faces. "What? Why are you looking at me like that? It says two dozen medium sliced loaves and four dozen rolls on my list. I can't help it if someone has messed up." She went back to her flower arrangement.

"Look! Let's just decide what we want and I'll go and get it," I said, wearily. "But for heaven's sake be quick; we can't afford to mess around any more. The time is slipping by."

It was true. There was still so much to do and now I had to go rushing off to the food store.

Another problem awaited me on my return. This time it was the fridge, it wasn't working properly. David was on his hands and knees peering at the works.

"It's simply too old. I believe the hall committee is in the process of buying another one," he said, looking up at me.

"That's all very well, but what are we going to do in the meantime? All this cooked meat will be spoiled if we leave it out in the heat." My patience was fast wearing thin. Perhaps a surprise party for Christine hadn't been such a good idea after all.

Jean came to the rescue, or at least her parents did. It appeared they had a lightweight fridge in their caravan. "It's small, but it might do for today."

I didn't care how small it was, it was a Godsend. Jean and I went off to find the fridge.

I was dreading my return to the hall. It seemed that every time I walked in I was met with trouble. This time was no exception. Ann, suddenly startled when a balloon suddenly burst, had dropped a large tray of glasses. She was in the process of brushing up the pieces.

"I'm not sure we'll have enough now. What do you think?" she asked.

"Would now be a good time to mention we're short of cutlery?"

"And plates?"

"Has anyone thought about serviettes?"

"This salmon doesn't smell right. Do you think it's off?"

Voices came at me from all directions. "I don't know and I don't care," I yelled. Why was everything going so terribly wrong? Calming down a little, I suggested that we all brought some cutlery and glasses from our homes when we came back that evening.

We worked quietly for the rest of the afternoon and by late afternoon we seemed to be getting to the stage when I thought we could relax, despite several of the balloons bursting due to the heat and the net falling down twice.

At that point I suggested it might be a good idea if we all went home to change. "But we'd better come straight back in case there's another catastrophe."

"Why don't you come to the party, David?" I asked. "You've been such a help today, it seems a shame to miss out on all the fun."

"I'm not sure I'll be able to stand the pace." His blue eyes twinkled. "The party hasn't even started and I feel dizzy already. I've fallen off the ladder once and nearly passed out twice while blowing up the balloons. I shudder to think what might happen once it's in full swing."

I suddenly felt guilty. I had noticed he'd gone cross-eyed a couple of times, but I'd merely believed him to be fooling around. What if he had fainted?

Just then Helen, who was rummaging in a cupboard, called out. "Look what I've found! It's a gadget for blowing up balloons."

I pushed David out of the door before he exploded. "Come back when you've showered and changed, you'll feel much better, I promise." Giving a final glance at the hall, I pulled the blinds and left.

When we came back, a further nail-biting situation awaited us. A burst water main had caused lengthy traffic diversions to be put into place. Fortunately, the guests arrived with a few minutes to spare.

It was almost time for the surprise. We all stood in the darkened hall hardly daring to say a word. I glanced at David and smiled. He wasn't really so bad after all, at least he had given me a lift to make sure I wouldn't be late and I must say, he washed and brushed up very well. Perhaps I had misjudged him.

Looking around the hall, I gave a sigh of relief. Everything was ready. The balloon net had finally agreed to stay aloft, the hall was beautifully decked out, the buffet looked delicious and we had managed to find enough glasses, cutlery and plates at the back of the cupboard. Even Jerry's music was what we wanted. I felt really confident about the evening; what could possibly go wrong now…?

But, at that very moment, a small voice at the back of the hall piped up, "Did anyone think to invite Christine?"

Reason to Celebrate

"Oh my goodness, I don't believe it." Madge sat down and put on her spectacles before reading the letter again. But it was true; the local planning office was informing her that Mr. James Armstrong of The Grange had applied for permission to open a supermarket in the village. Any objections should be put in writing.

Objections! Of course she had objections. What would become of her grocery shop if a supermarket were to open? She looked out into the street towards the other three shops that served the small village. Had they received a copy of the letter? A supermarket would affect them too.

Though James Armstrong and his wife had lived in the village for a number of years, they'd never fitted in. They had always refused to join in any local activities, declaring such pastimes were childish and beneath their dignity.

James, being a wealthy businessman, rather fancied himself as a country gentleman. He was often seen striding around the village as though he owned it. His wife usually drove around in a large open-topped car, showing off her designer clothes.

Madge had never been keen on either of them. She didn't like their hoity-toity attitude towards the villagers. They seldom shopped locally, much preferring to have their groceries delivered by one of the large stores in the city. "They have so much more to offer," James had said on more than one occasion. "Why anyone would want to shop locally beats me."

So then why on earth should James Armstrong want to open a supermarket? But on reflection, the reason was obvious. The village was slowly increasing in size and James wanted a piece of the action. Families were coming here from the city in search of a more peaceful lifestyle.

With modern machinery available to them, farmers no longer retained large numbers of farmhands. This being so, many of the small cottages, which had once housed them, had been sold off. Even lowly barns and other farm buildings, were being converted into 'homes for the more discerning families', as the estate agent put it.

But even more alarming, John Pearce the local small builder had also seized the opportunity to make himself some money and was seeking permission to build a dozen houses on a piece of ground at the edge of the village.

He himself had kept very quiet about it, avoiding awkward questions from the locals. But Madge had read the planning application notice in the local paper a couple of weeks ago.

She sighed. It was such a shame. That land had been a children's playground for as long as she could remember. It would soon be lost if John Pearce got his way. The village was changing and all for the worse. Now there was to be a supermarket. What would be next?

Fred from the bakery next door strode into the shop, interrupting her thoughts.

"You've seen it then." He nodded towards the letter in her hand. "What do you make of it?"

"Naturally I'm unhappy about it. But what can we do?"

"What we need is a really good reason why the village doesn't want a supermarket." Fred banged his fist down hard on the counter making Madge jump.

"Or an even better reason why the village doesn't need a new housing estate." Madge added, thoughtfully. "Without the housing project, James may not want a supermarket."

"Yes, you're right there. I never was in favour of the new houses even though they might have been good for business. They'll spoil the whole character of the village. I'd hate that. Look, I'd better go. A customer has gone into my shop. Let's all get together this evening and have a discussion."

Madge agreed and once Fred left the shop, she tried to think of something to put an end to the housing scheme. But she failed to come up with anything. Unless one of the others had a solution, the project would be allowed to go ahead.

Looking at her watch, she realised Jean would be here shortly. Jean was a cheerful sort, who came in three days a week to help out. No doubt she would be interested to hear about the supermarket. Madge put the kettle on. News like this needed to be pondered over tea and biscuits.

Over their tea Madge told Jean about the letter and how the four shopkeepers were getting together that evening to discuss the situation.

"I agree with you," said Jean. "Putting an end to the housing scheme would stop the supermarket. But the four of you arguing with the planning department won't change anything. If you really mean business, you need to get the whole village involved."

Jean was right; the village should be involved. But Madge wondered if anyone would be really interested? Some may not mind new homes in the village.

"Of course they'll mind." Jean looked determined. "They'd be fools not to. This is their village for heaven's sake. It'll be spoiled if they don't do something about it. New homes mean more traffic and then what? Before you know it we'll have a large filling station and so it goes on. But they all need to know what's going on. Not many read planning applications."

Madge thought about John. He was building the new homes; surely he wouldn't spoil the village. He would have to live with the outcome. But Jean almost exploded when she mentioned it.

"John Pearce won't be living here once the houses are finished. I have it on good authority he's planning to move out immediately they're sold."

Madge looked at Jean in disbelief. "Move out? Are you sure? I can't believe it. John's lived here all his life. We were at school together."

"Of course I'm sure." Jean poured out another cup of tea. "My son has been seeing rather a lot of his daughter and she was telling him about her father's plans. And there's something else that might interest you. Only last night, I heard that the houses won't stop at twelve. There'll be more than four times that number before he's finished. He's going to make a packet and run. So what do you think about that?"

Madge was fuming. So they were going to be stuck with a large housing estate, a supermarket and that was only the beginning. Other builders would soon jump on the bandwagon.

However, Madge wasn't able to tell Jean what she really thought, as the first of the morning's customers came in.

Leaving Jean to hold the fort, Madge dashed across to the other shops and told the owners what she had learned. Between them they agreed to inform all their customers that a meeting would be held in the church hall on Friday evening. Being all of three days away, gave them the time to let everyone know.

"I'll call on old Mr. Amos," said Fred. "I know he'll probably fall asleep during the meeting, but he likes to be involved in anything important."

Madge nodded. Mr. Amos was a much loved and respected member of the village. During his long life he had fought in two world wars and had worked his way through the education ranks, finally becoming vice-chancellor at a leading university.

Nowadays, he spent much of his time sitting in the garden watching the world go by. Or perhaps it would be more truthful to say sleeping, as the world passed him by.

The next morning, Madge had a visit from James Armstrong. He had heard about the meeting to oppose his supermarket and was extremely angry.

"What are you playing at? The village deserve better than the likes of this." He waved his hands around, indicating he was referring to Madge's shop. "I'll give them more choice. That's what people want today, woman, choice. Not what little you stock here."

His face had gone quite red, Madge was alarmed he might cause himself some mischief. "Calm yourself, Mr. Armstrong. That's what the meeting is about; an opportunity for the people to choose what they want."

"Once I tell them my prices will be cheaper, they'll agree to my supermarket," James insisted. "Just you wait and see. This village will have reason to celebrate on Friday evening." He turned and left the shop, slamming the door behind him.

Madge was concerned James could be right. People always wanted cheaper prices. If he were to buy in bulk, he could afford to sell the goods more cheaply. But would he? After the first week or two, would he raise the prices again, using inflation as an excuse?

Though John Pearce was unhappy about the village meeting, he was quietly confident that his application would be approved by the council. As far as they were concerned, it would bring in more community charges.

"Just think of it, Madge, brand new houses. Isn't it exciting?" It was obvious he was hoping his enthusiasm would rub off on her. With her on his side, the meeting would be a walkover. "Why you might even like one for yourself. Naturally as a friend from school days, I'd give you first choice and at a discount. They'll have lovely fitted kitchens and bathrooms. I can see you in one, can't you?"

But Madge was having none of it.

"No I can't," she retorted. "And you should be ashamed of yourself, building on that land. Children have played there for years, where will they go now?"

But he merely shrugged his shoulders and walked out. Madge knew he didn't care, after ruining the village, he was moving on.

The rest of the week was a nightmare. James took every opportunity to tell the gang of five, poor Jean having been added to their number, that they were all wasting their time. "You all have your heads stuck in the sand. You're all so pig-headed."

"Make your mind up, man; are we ostriches or pigs?" Fred called out on one occasion. They had all laughed, making James even more annoyed. But they all knew that he would still win if the council granted permission for the housing project.

Concerned about the proposed changes, the meeting attracted most of the village. Even old Mr. Amos turned up. Fred opened the meeting by thanking everyone for coming.

Madge looked at Mr. Amos and smiled. His eyes were shut; he had fallen asleep already. Just then the door burst open and James strode in, John followed close behind. "We're here because we have a right to be heard too. The villagers should hear all the facts."

Fred stepped down to make way for the two men. "You'd best say your piece then."

John spoke first, telling them the housing estate would be good for the village.

"How?" asked someone at the back.

"Well, it will bring new life to us all."

"What do you mean by 'us all'," Madge called out. "As I understand it, you're leaving once the project is completed."

John turned beetroot. He couldn't deny it.

"You idiot," hissed Mr. Armstrong. "How did that get out? Couldn't you keep your mouth shut?"

Pushing John out of the way, he looked down at the audience and smiled. "The housing will be a good thing for us all by bringing new and exciting businesses to the village; for instance, my supermarket." He paused and pointed at Madge and the others. "They're only looking out for themselves. My goods will be cheaper." After explaining a little more, he stepped down.

Fred asked if anyone objected to the housing project. Everyone put up their hand.

"That doesn't mean it won't go ahead," James yelled out in desperation. "Just because you can't move with the times, doesn't mean the project is wrong. Once the council decides in favour of it, my supermarket will..."

"John can't build on that land." Everyone looked towards Mr. Amos.

"Yes, we know," Fred explained gently. "That's why we're here. But I'm not sure we can stop the council from agreeing to John's proposals and..."

"No. You don't understand," Mr. Amos interrupted. "The council can't agree; the land doesn't belong to them." He paused and looked around the hall. "It belongs to all of you. It was bequeathed to the village over two hundred years ago by Thomas Hargrove, the then Lord of the Manor. A charter was established, which declares that the land cannot be sold or used for anything without the consent of every single member of the village."

Everyone was stunned. Pulling herself together, Madge asked if he was sure.

"Of course I'm sure. A copy of the document is in the library archives, but the original is held in London."

"Well I'll be a monkey's uncle," said Fred, slapping his knee. "Mr. Amos, I'm going to treat you to a large brandy across at the pub." He looked across at Madge. "I declare this meeting closed."

The community, delighted with the outcome, followed Fred down the lane to the pub. James and John sat down, they were speechless.

On reaching the door, Madge looked back at the two men. "Aren't you coming? After all, it was you who said we'd have reason to celebrate this evening. Though I must admit, I don't think this is quite what you had in mind."

Same Time on Friday?

Standing anxiously by the window, I watched a car turn the corner of the road. Could this be Mr. Jenkins now? But it wasn't and I breathed a sigh of relief. I had been given a few minutes reprieve. Why was I being so stupid? It was only a driving lesson for heaven's sake!

The lessons were a twenty-first birthday gift from my friends. "The instructor comes highly recommended, Wendy," they'd said. "We're sure you'll both get along famously."

I recalled how I had looked forward to my first lesson, only to be disappointed when Mr. Jenkins seemed to take an instant dislike to me. Perhaps I had expected too much, believing he would show a little sympathy to someone on their first lesson.

But instead, he had directed me to one of the busiest roads in town. Then when I stalled the car he acted like a man possessed. For goodness sake, surely I wasn't the first person he had encountered to stall the engine?

At the end of the lesson, he told me how the last hour had been a remarkable experience and like a fool I had thanked him.

"It was not meant as a compliment, Miss Goodwin," he'd said peering over the top of his glasses. "Lost as to how else to describe the experience, I simply meant that it had been... remarkable." Finally, after giving me a sarcastic grin, he'd added rather pompously, "Same time on Friday, Miss Goodwin?"

Red faced and in tears, I'd leapt out of the car and hurried indoors.

My second lesson had been no better. Taking me to the busiest round-a-bout on the by-pass, he had told me to turn right. "You do know your left from your right don't you, Miss Goodwin?" he'd smirked.

Approaching the round-a-bout, he told me to move over to the right of the carriageway. But I had only begun to turn the wheel, when he yelled, "Not that far over, girl. You'll have us on the wrong side of the road."

But worse was to come. Because he had made me so nervous, once I got onto the wretched round-a-bout, I couldn't get off. I'll never forget it. There we were, going round and round and round.

Naturally my friends were annoyed at his behaviour; one of them wanted to report him to his superiors and demand a refund. But I intervened; not wanting to cause trouble. Besides, it was like I was returning their gift.

Nevertheless, there was no doubt something had to be done; otherwise I would lose my sanity.

Sue suggested that we make a few discreet enquiries about Mr. Jenkins. This seemed a good idea. Perhaps someone could throw some light on his attitude towards me.

It only took a few days to learn that several women, having been assigned to Mr. Jenkins, had experienced the same treatment. However, it appeared he was totally different when a man was in the driving seat.

This led us to the conclusion that Mr. Jenkins didn't like women drivers and making their lessons intolerable was a sure way of putting them off driving for life.

My friends and I were furious, immediately deciding we should do something about it; but what? We couldn't prove anything. In the meantime, my refusing to give in meant I was stuck with the wretched man.

By the end of my third lesson I was a nervous wreck. "Same time on Friday, Miss Goodwin?" he said with that same stupid smirk on his face.

I nodded, but deep down, I wondered if I was doing the right thing. That evening, while seriously thinking about cancelling my lessons, my lovely brother, David, telephoned. He was seeking a room at my house for the next week.

It appeared his firm had suddenly asked him to stand in for a colleague at a series of meetings in a nearby town and he was hoping to save a little on his expenses. "Though I insist on paying for my keep," he'd added.

Naturally, I had agreed to him staying with me. How could I refuse? Besides, it would be fun seeing him again; since he had moved to a firm in the north, we seldom saw each other. But I was on the point of telling him I didn't want any money, when an idea formed in my mind.

"David," I'd said, as sweetly as possible. "Perhaps we could do a deal. Would you take me out for a few driving lessons in your car?" I paused. "Well, a lot of driving lessons, actually."

"I thought you were having lessons," he said.

"Yes I am, but if you were to take me out for a drive every day for the next week, I think I would pick it up a lot more quickly."

I didn't want to tell him about Mr. Jenkins' attitude. He may have wanted to punch him on the nose.

So every day last week, I had a lesson with David, who I found to be much more patient than Mr. Jenkins. He explained everything very carefully and even showed me how the engine worked.

Though I thought that was going a bit over the top, I listened intently. Mr. Jenkins might just throw in a question or two to catch me out.

By the time David went back north, I felt much more confident. I could go around round-a-bouts, reverse around corners, and do emergency stops. It was as though I had been born doing them. He had even quizzed me on the Highway Code.

So why was I standing here waiting for Mr. Jenkins, still feeling so nervous. Surely he couldn't find fault with me today.

Another car turned the corner at the end of the road. My stomach flipped over as I recognised the figure behind the wheel. Any minute now he would pull up at my front door.

I took a couple of deep breaths and went out to meet him. "Good morning, Mr. Jenkins," I said as cheerfully as possible. "It's a lovely day isn't it?"

"Yes, it is at the moment, Miss Goodwin." He sighed. "But no doubt you'll soon spoil it for me. Get into the car please."

I climbed into the driver's seat and made myself comfortable.

Fastening my seat belt, I checked the position of the seat and adjusted the mirror. I was not going to allow him the satisfaction of saying that I had forgotten anything.

He took out a large note pad. "When you're quite ready I'd like you to move off to the end of the road and turn right."

So far, so good; turning right would take me into a quiet lane. At least I was being given time to gather my thoughts.

"We're going to do a three point turn today, something you no doubt will find difficult. Nevertheless it's an important manoeuver, especially when taking your test; should you get that far, of course. I do have my doubts."

"Really, Mr. Jenkins? I thought I was doing rather well. I'm quite enjoying my lessons." I turned away and grinned to myself. Mr. Jenkins' face was a picture.

He was probably wondering how anyone could enjoy what he was putting me through. But for my part, I was even more determined to carry on.

Remembering all that David had taught me, I drove a few yards towards the end of the road and signalled to turn right.

"Stop! Stop! Pull into the side and turn off the engine."

I did as he asked. What could possibly be wrong now? I had barely moved.

"There's no need to signal so early, especially when there is no one behind."

"But only last week you said that I should always indicate early to let the other drivers know my intentions. Even though, I might add, there was no one behind at the time. You said it was a good habit to get into."

"That was a totally different situation. We were on a main road. Someone might have pulled out of a turning. Anyway, I'm the instructor; don't you argue with me, young lady. I can see that you are not cut out for driving. Why don't you call it a day and take the bus?"

I gritted my teeth. "I'm not ready to give up yet, Mr. Jenkins. As I told you earlier, I'm enjoying these lessons. Shall I try again?"

"Very well Miss Goodwin, if you must. Pull out and turn right at the end of the road then stop the car. We'll tackle the three point turn; you shouldn't be too much of a hazard to anyone there. But I want you to know I shall be taking lots of notes today and will inform you of my honest opinion at the end of the lesson. Shall we proceed?"

By now I was furious. He had all but admitted that he wanted me to quit. Well not yet, my old fruit, I'll show you a thing or two.

I looked in my mirror, indicated and pulled out. Proceeding down the road, I signalled my intention to turn right and moved over.

Mr. Jenkins sighed, but didn't say anything. I guessed he was trying to unnerve me again. But by now, I was determined not to let him get to me. Enough was enough. Two could play at that game.

I turned right and pulled up at the kerb, but instead of waiting for his instruction, I did a three point turn. If I say it myself it was perfect. But I didn't stop there, having started this I was determined to see it through and, without him noticing, I removed the key that mobilized his controls.

Not waiting for his comments, I proceeded towards the by-pass and the dreaded round-a-bout. I indicated right and moved over. At the round-a-bout, I moved gently into the traffic and once round turned off and headed towards a quiet residential area.

All the while Mr. Jenkins was sliding around the seat, his feet stamping up and down on his redundant controls. "Miss Goodwin, what do you think you're doing? Turn around immediately."

"Oh, I see, Mr. Jenkins. You'd like me to go around again?" After making sure that there was no traffic behind, I pulled the car to a halt and did another three point turn before proceeding back to the round-a-bout.

"Miss Goodwin, have you gone mad?"

"But you wanted me to do it again." By this time I was back at the round-a-bout and signalling right. "Of course once I'm out there, I'll indicate that I want to go all the way around," I said, beginning to enjoy myself.

Having done a full circle, I turned off and headed towards the quiet streets. I could tell Mr. Jenkins was furious. Banging his notepad down onto the dashboard, he yelled. "Stop this car, I want..."

The rest of his words were lost as, after glancing in all the mirrors, I thrust my feet hard onto both the brake and clutch pedals. The car came to an immediate halt, throwing the instructor forward in his seat. "There now, Mr. Jenkins, wasn't that just the perfect emergency stop? You had better make a note of that."

"Miss Goodwin, I think we should go back..."

"And do it again." I interrupted. "Yes, you're absolutely right. That's a good decision. You want to see whether I'm capable of pulling it off twice."

The colour was beginning to drain from his face. "No, I meant…"

But I didn't give him time to finish, putting the car into reverse gear, I did a neat job of reversing around the corner. Pulling out, I drove up to the end of the road and did another three point turn.

"Miss Goodwin, It isn't necessary to do it again I…"

"Oh but it is, Mr. Jenkins. I want you to be quite clear in your mind that I am capable of this manoeuver." And without another word I drove down the road only to come to another sudden halt.

I tried not to laugh as Mr. Jenkins wiped his face with his handkerchief. But I wasn't finished yet. I still had to drive home. Reversing around the corner again, I pulled out and drove towards the round-a-bout. I could almost feel Mr. Jenkins cringing as we drew near.

"What a pity, I only have to do a left here. But perhaps you'd like me to go around one full circle." And without waiting for an answer, I did just that. Mr. Jenkins put his hand over his eyes.

"There now," I said. "Wasn't that beautiful? I hope you made a note of that, too."

Out of the corner of my eye, I saw him peeping between his fingers.

I drove towards my home, but there was more to come. Checking that the road was clear, I did a three point turn, reversed around a corner and finally, an emergency stop outside my door.

By this time, the instructor was almost under his seat. "I really think I'm getting the hang of it now, don't you?" I said, sliding out of the car. But before slamming the door shut, I leant inside and, smiling sweetly, added, "Same time on Friday, Mr. Jenkins?"

The Last Pea on the Plate

"Would you mind if I sat here?"

Jane looked up to see a young man gazing down at her. He was balancing a tray of food rather awkwardly on one hand, while clutching a bulky briefcase with the other.

"No, go ahead." She quickly slid the condiments to one side to allow him more room.

Glancing around the café, she noticed there were still a few empty tables and thought it strange he had chosen to sit here. Most people preferred to sit alone.

Placing the tray on the table, he nodded towards the window. "It's rather a nice day today."

"Yes, I suppose it is," she replied, without looking. She was too busy noting how attractive he was. Clean shaven, smartly dressed and...

"I'm Bob, by the way," he said, interrupting her thoughts. He held out his hand. "Pleased to meet you."

"Thank you." Though she took his hand, she didn't give her name.

"I like coming here, the food is always very good," he said after removing his coat.

"Yes," replied Jane. She cringed. Why couldn't she think of something sparkling and witty to say? Here she was sitting opposite this gorgeous guy, who obviously wanted to talk and yet she couldn't think of one amusing thing to say.

There was an embarrassing silence.

For heaven's sake, Jane, she scolded herself. He must be a tiny bit interested in you to have sat here in the first place. Say something – anything!

"Haven't I seen you in here before?" Bob asked, suddenly. "Don't you usually have a couple of friends with you?"

Jane sank back in her chair. So that was it. He was only interested in her friends. She should have guessed. It was true; she often met two friends here at lunchtime, but they were both on holiday this week. She sighed. She had to admit she couldn't blame the guy. Jenny and Lucy were very attractive young ladies. They would have charmed him off his feet by now.

Obviously Bob had seen them all together and had decided to join her simply because he thought they would be here shortly. Well today, he was in for a shock – he was stuck with her. All the same, it was disappointing he should merely look on her as a means to an end. But then she should be used to it. It was a regular occurrence in her life.

"Yes," she replied, trying to hide the disappointment in her voice. "I do meet my friends here occasionally."

She refrained from telling him they weren't coming today. Let him find out for himself! Besides, she would be leaving shortly.

"What is it with that pea?" he asked, a few minutes later. "You've been pushing it around your plate for ages.

"It's the last pea on the plate," she replied, keeping her head down.

"So?" The inclination in his voice told her it was a question rather than a statement.

She looked up and shrugged. "It's simple. When I got this meal, there were several peas on the plate. Most of them were scooped up onto my fork earlier. But this one got left behind, so I'm making sure it gets picked up now."

"I see." He paused and shook his head. "No; actually, I don't see. Does it really matter if one pea gets thrown away?"

"Of course it does," she said, indignantly.

"Why?" He pushed his empty plate to one side.

"Are you really interested?" Jane asked. She cocked her head on one side and scrutinised him. He didn't look the sort who would be concerned about a solitary pea lying on an empty plate.

"More curious, I suppose." He smiled. "But either way, I'd like to know."

"I tend to think all growing things have feelings." She pointed to her plate. "That one pea, like all the others, went through a long process. It began life by being sown in the ground. Over the course of the year it was fed and watered – growing up with other peas in a pod. Finally they were picked and shipped off to market. Then one day a cook removed the peas from their pods and cooked them. That means, if I don't eat this one last pea, all that growing and ripening will have been for nothing. It will feel alone – separated from the others and worthless. It's much the same with baked beans."

"Baked Beans!" Bob grinned. "How did baked beans get into the equation?"

"Because, again, they go through a similar process. But in their case, one or two beans often get stuck at the bottom of the can, which means unless you shake it really hard, they won't even reach the pan. Therefore, like peas left on a plate, their destiny is unfulfilled."

"Well I have to say, you have a vivid imagination." He laughed. "I've never heard anything like it. "How on earth did you come up with a thought like that?"

"Now you're making fun of me."

"No, I'm not. Honest, cross my heart." He stopped laughing. "I'm really interested."

Jane looked down at the pea on her plate. "Because I see myself as one of those little peas," she said thoughtfully. "I was cared for by my family – fed and watered if you like, until I ripened and was let loose to find my own way." She sighed. "But I always seem to be the last pea on the plate. I'm the one that gets left behind." She lifted her head. "For example – aren't you're only sitting with me, because you hoped I'd introduce you to my glamorous friends. Well I'll tell you something – they aren't coming. They're away all this week, so…"

She stopped abruptly. What was she doing? How could she have poured her heart out to a complete stranger? She stood up to leave, but he caught her arm and pulled her back.

"Is that what you think?" When she didn't answer, Bob tried again. "Do you really believe I asked to join you, simply to meet your friends?"

"Well didn't you?" Jane retorted.

"No, not at all." He paused. "I wanted to talk to you." He glanced at his watch. "I have to go now, I'm due at a meeting at two o'clock, but I'd like to see you again."

"Well, I'm here most lunch times," she said grudgingly. She wasn't entirely convinced. This meeting he had suddenly mentioned was a little too convenient. It sounded more of a get out clause to her.

"Fine, I'll see you tomorrow." Bob turned to go, but then he hesitated. "Promise you'll be here."

Jane watched him leave the café, her eyes following him until he disappeared from sight. She had agreed to come tomorrow – but had she done the right thing?

Back at the office, Jane couldn't focus on her job. Even her colleagues noticed her lack of concentration. After a great deal of quizzing, she told them about Bob and their impending meeting, though she didn't say where it would take place.

One or two made some spiteful remarks, saying she was stupid to think he would turn up. Jane was left wishing she hadn't said anything. What if they were right? She had to admit, back at the café, she'd had doubts of her own. But she had talked herself into believing him.

The next morning, Jane kept looking at the office clock. The time seemed to drag. However the pointers finally relented and moved to one o'clock. Grabbing her coat, she headed for the café.

During the long morning, she had wondered what she might talk about when she met Bob. Though she couldn't bring anything original to mind, one thing was certain; she wasn't going to mention peas! She winced when she thought about her speech the day before.

Bob wasn't at the café when she arrived. She went to the counter and selected her meal – declining the offer of peas. The service seemed to be slower than usual. It seemed the lady taking the money was chatting to every customer. At last it was her turn.

Choosing a prominent table by the window, Jane kept watching for Bob to turn the corner at the bottom of the street. Yet there was no sign of him. She recalled he came in after her yesterday, but as the time passed, she knew he hadn't been this late.

She closed her eyes. He wasn't coming. Despite his reassurances, he wasn't interested in her after all. She had been right; it was her two friends he had wanted to meet. No doubt he would turn up next week when they were back from holiday.

Tears welled in her eyes. All she wanted to do was to go home. How could she face her colleagues at the office? Perhaps she could say she had come over feeling ill. But they would guess what had really happened. Heading back to the office, she tried to think of a plausible excuse for Bob's non-appearance.

"Like I said, Bob phoned my mobile to say he was tied up." It was the only thing she could think of when she was cross-examined by her friends. "He apologised, but said he would meet me another day. These things do happen, especially when you're in business." She then made her escape to cloakroom, before anyone could say anything further.

"Bob stood you up, didn't he?" Ann had followed Jane into the ladies room.

"No! Not at all! Like I said he called me on my mobile and…" Jane stopped. Ann was holding up a mobile phone.

"You left this behind. I ran downstairs after you, but you'd gone."

"Yes, all right, he didn't turn up." Jane bit her lip. "I should have expected it. But you know, deep down I wanted to believe him." She sighed. "Please don't tell the others."

"Of course I won't." Ann put her arm around her friend. "You're such a lovely person, Jane, one of these days you'll meet a man who realises what a gem he has in you." She smiled. Now come on, we'd better get back to work before someone notices we're missing."

Jane was thankful when it was time to go home. Though no one had actually come out and said so, she felt sure some of her colleagues hadn't believed her story about Bob not being able to get away.

As she made her way out of the office the following lunchtime, Jane wasn't sure whether to go to the same café. The thought of seeing Bob filled her with dread. Would he smile awkwardly before turning back to his meal? Perhaps he wouldn't even acknowledge her. On the other hand, if she went somewhere else she wouldn't have to see him at all. There were plenty of other snack bars to choose from. Maybe that would be the best idea.

Yet despite her intentions, her feet headed in the direction of her usual café. Her heart was in her mouth as she glanced around the interior, but thankfully Bob wasn't there. She sighed with relief. Hopefully he wouldn't come in at all. She had almost finished her meal when she heard a voice behind her.

"Thank goodness, I've caught you. I thought you might have left by now." Bob dropped his briefcase to the floor and sat down beside her. He looked flushed, as though he had been running. "Sorry about yesterday, but I had a rush job in Edinburgh."

Jane looked puzzled. "I… I just thought you'd changed your mind…"

"Didn't you get my message?" Bob asked.

"What message?"

"At the meeting yesterday afternoon, I learned I had to take an immediate trip to Scotland, "he explained. "I didn't know how to get in touch with you, so this morning I phoned the manageress of this café and asked if she would tell every young woman who was having peas with their lunch that Bob couldn't come, but I'd be here today." He laughed. "From her tone I think she thought I was mad, but it was the only thing I could think of. I didn't even have your name. Anyway, I persuaded her I wasn't a lunatic and she agreed to do it – she must be a romantic at heart. But you say she didn't tell you."

"No." Jane laughed, recalling how the lady on the till had struck up a conversation with most of the customers, but not her. "But then I avoided the peas yesterday."

"You must have thought…" Bob broke off. For a moment he looked solemn. "Thank goodness you came here today – you could easily have chosen another cafe. I might never have seen you again." He sighed. "Well before we both have to rush back to work, can we make a dinner date for this evening? Where do you live? I'll pick you up at seven." He glanced at her plate. "And what about that last pea?"

Jane was walking on air, as she went back into the office. Bob really liked her after all. "For the first time in my life, I'm not the last pea on the plate," she murmured, happily.

"What's that about peas?" Ann raised her eyebrows.

"Remind me to tell you about it sometime," laughed Jane. "It's a long story."

The Little Fairy

Martha looked out the window; her face glowing with satisfaction. Over the last few months, she and her son, David had worked very hard in the garden. Both determined to make it look exactly the way her husband, Ben had planned it.

She waved as David's car pulled onto the drive. "I'm sorry I'm late, Mum," he said, getting out of his car. "I had hoped to be here long before now, but the traffic was so bad today." He looked around the garden. "I see you've been busy again; I wish you'd waited until I got here. You know, you're doing far too much."

"Nonsense! I'm quite enjoying it. Besides, I need to do this for your father's sake. We both know how much time he spent during the winter months planning it all out; I want to bring his vision to life."

"I know, Mum," David said gently. "But I worry that you're overdoing it. Dad wouldn't want you to work so hard."

Martha didn't answer. She was recalling how Ben had always made the most of his garden. Every summer the neighbours could only look on in envy, as his beautiful garden began to unfold.

She smiled to herself when she thought of how he spent hours talking to his plants; gently coaxing them into bloom. He would never admit it to any one, not even her, but she knew it to be true. She had often heard him when she'd gone down the garden to fetch him for his dinner or take him a cup of tea. However, when she asked who he was talking to, he'd simply smile and tap his nose, saying, "A little fairy, Martha; just a little fairy."

Once out in his beloved garden he lost all track of time. At mealtimes, Martha had to seek him out; left to his own devices, he would have starved a long time ago. But she never complained; it was good seeing him do something he loved. Besides, she delighted in the garden being so full of beautiful flowers.

She thought back to those warm summer afternoons when they both took tea on the patio surrounded by the delightful blooms. And then there were the evenings, when after dinner they'd sit side by side drinking in the fragrance of the night-scented flowers. She had been looking forward to it again this year, until that fateful day when Ben had suddenly taken it into his head to pull out the old tree stump.

She bit her lip at the thought. That wretched stump, it had been there all these years. Why couldn't he have let it be? Instead, he had spent hours digging around the roots before throwing down his garden tools and began heaving at it. She had gone to call him in for dinner when she'd seen him lying on the ground, motionless.

The ambulance people were quick to respond. They had rushed him to the local hospital, trying to revive him all the while.

"Your husband has had a serious heart-attack," the doctor had said. He told her that Ben needed major surgery and would have to be moved to the large hospital in the city.

After the operation, she and David were informed that he wasn't responding and his chances of recovery were very slim. If he were younger, perhaps things would be different, but at his age...

Tears ran down her cheeks as it all came flooding back to her; Ben lying there with all those tubes and wires attached to his body. It hadn't looked like him at all. Not being able to bear it any longer, she'd run blindly from the hospital and had never gone back.

She looked across to where the tree stump had been. It was gone now of course. David had been so angry at what had happened to his father, he'd torn it out and burned it.

"Mum, are you all right?" David's voice broke into her thoughts. He looked anxious.

"Yes, of course I am, dear" she replied, reaching out to him. "I was just thinking about your father." She wiped away the tears. "So tell me, how's my beautiful grandson?"

"Daniel's great, Mum," David's face broke into smiles. "He's cut his first tooth. Sandy says that he did it without all the fuss babies usually make when their teeth start coming through." David looked so proud standing there.

Martha smiled to herself. She recalled Ben being the same when David was a baby. According to him, David was the smartest child around. It was such a pity that she hadn't been able to have any more children. But there now, she mustn't dwell on the past. "That's wonderful news son. I'm so looking forward to seeing him next week."

"Yes, Sandy was just remarking that it's been a while since she and the baby were last here."

"Yes, it was just after your father..." she broke off unable to finish.

"Well now, what do we need to do next?" David said, quickly diverting the subject away from his father's heart-attack. He glanced around the garden; he had already done most of the heavy work. "I think it's time to put in the bedding plants. Perhaps we should go down to the garden centre tomorrow morning to choose some from Dad's list. I know there are plants growing in the greenhouse, but I don't think there'll be nearly enough; not for what Dad had in mind, anyway."

Martha agreed. She had done her best with the seeds, but pricking out the seedlings had been too fiddly for her. The tiny plants were so delicate; many had simply dropped through her arthritic fingers and landed on the floor. She had marvelled at how Ben, with his large, strong hands, had been able to treat them with such loving care.

"That's a good idea," she said. "Your father always said that if you don't choose them early, you are left with plants no one else wants.

"All right, Mum, I'll call for you and we'll go together. Have Dad's list ready and I'll pick you up first thing. I don't think there's anything more we can do today, it's starting to rain. Besides, you seem to have finished it all."

Once David had left, Martha locked the greenhouse and after a final glance around the garden, she went indoors.

The next morning David took his mother to the garden centre. There were many pretty plants to choose from, but Martha insisted that they stuck rigidly to her husband's list. "The garden must look exactly as he planned it," she said. "We mustn't be sidetracked."

Though it took some time, they managed to find all the plants on Ben's list. When they arrived back home, Martha told David that it was time for him to go and spend some time with his wife and son.

But he wasn't having any of that. "I know that once I've gone you'll set about planting all these on your own," he said. "Sandy knows how much this means to us so she won't be expecting me home for a while yet."

David insisted that she should leave him to do much of the work, saying, "I could really do with a nice cup of tea, Mum. Why don't you go and put the kettle on?"

Martha knew that he was worried about her and didn't argue. Besides, she was grateful for the help. Though she would never admit to it, David was right; she was doing far too much. Each evening over the past few weeks, she had been forced to retire long before her usual bedtime.

By the time Martha got back with a tray of tea and biscuits, David had already made a start. "It's looking good son," she said. "I can see the patterns taking shape already."

In his plans, Ben had divided the garden into different shapes. When all the plants were in full bloom those shapes would magically turn into butterflies and birds whose colourful wings would shimmer in the summer breeze.

"Yes," said David, joining his mother. "It's certainly going to be a picture this year." He sat down on the garden chair and took a sip of tea. "I think Dad wanted this to be his masterpiece. He'd certainly planned everything down to the very last detail."

Once the tea was finished, David went back to the planting, telling his mother to put her feet up for a while. "I can manage here; please mum, I'd like you to take it easy today."

Though Martha protested strongly, she was really quite relieved. She had never realized that gardening was such hard work. Or was it that she was just getting old? Old age seemed to have crept up when she wasn't looking.

David spent the rest of the day working in the garden. He told her he would try to finish the planting before going home that evening as rain was forecast for the following day. "Naturally I'll water in the plants tonight," he said. "But I've often heard Dad say, there's nothing like a good shower of rain to bed them in properly."

By the end of the day the planting was finished. But before leaving, David reminded his mother that he would be bringing Sandy and the baby for a visit the following Friday.

The week wore on and as Friday drew near, Martha grew excited at the prospect of seeing her grandson again. David dropped Sandy off before going on to the office, saying he would be back with a surprise just after lunch. Martha welcomed Sandy and Daniel, remarking several times on how much the baby had grown since she had last seen him.

Sandy looked around the garden in amazement. "David's been so worried about you. He believes you've been doing too much; I can see now that he was right." She gently placed her hand on her mother-in-law's arm. "You know Ben wouldn't have wanted you to go to all this trouble."

"I know, my dear. But I wanted to do it for him. It would've been the first year that his garden hadn't been tended properly. I simply couldn't let that happen; not when he had been so excited about the plans he'd made."

Shortly after lunch, David's car pulled up onto the drive. By the time Martha and Sandy had reached the door, he was pulling a large suitcase out of the boot.

Tears ran down Martha's cheeks as the passenger door opened and Ben stepped out. Martha ran across to him. "Oh Ben! My dearest Ben. What a wonderful surprise. I just can't believe it. The doctor said you'd be away at the nursing home for several weeks yet. It's so good to have you home."

David stood back as his parents were reunited. Sandy drew close to him and he put his arm around her.

"My darling Martha," said Ben hugging his wife. "When I felt those terrible pains all those months ago, I thought I'd never see you again. But here I am, home again; fit and well." He looked around the garden in amazement. "It looks wonderful. But how... who did all this?"

Only too happy to have her husband back where he belonged, Martha simply smiled happily and said, "Why Ben, my dear, it must have been your little fairy!"

The Number 57 Bus

Alice slowly ran her finger down the list of contents in the book. Usually she looked forward to her lunch break. It was a time when she could take a book from the shelves of the library where she worked and lose herself in the pages.

A book from the adventure section might take her in search of buried treasure on some small deserted island, or bring her into conflict with the raging waters of the Colorado River as it rushed through the Grand Canyon.

But it was the travel section that really interested her the most. There was no limit to the wonderful places she could visit without moving from her quiet corner in the library.

Today however, Alice found that even the lure of a sun-drenched beach on a Caribbean Island could do nothing to help her present mood and she shut her book with a loud snap.

"Oh, there you are."

Alice jumped at the sound of the voice. She hadn't heard anyone come into the library. Usually the bell above the door rang so loudly that even when lost in the depth of the Amazon, she heard it jangling. But today, she had heard nothing at all.

"I'm sorry if I disturbed you," the voice continued. "But the girl on the desk said you would know where I could find something to help me with my research on... I say, you're not thinking of going there are you? You're a lucky lady."

Alice looked up at the man in front of her. Her mind flew back to a few weeks ago when Anne, the part-time girl who covered the lunch period, had helped him fill in the enrolment form. "A real gentleman," she had said over a cup of tea. "You don't meet many like that these days."

Alice reckoned he must be about her age... or perhaps a little older. But his smart clothes and his hair, greying at the temples, gave him a rather distinguished look.

"May I?" he asked, interrupting her thoughts. He pointed towards the book.

She nodded and watched him as he flicked through the pages.

"Yes, it looks very nice. I'm sure you'll enjoy your stay on the island," he said, handing the book back to her.

"No. You don't understand. I'm not going there," said Alice. "Not at my time of life. I simply enjoy spending my lunch break reading about all those wonderful, faraway places."

"What do you mean, at your time of life?" said the gentleman sitting down beside her. "A young woman like you should get out there and see the world."

Alice laughed. "You're a flatterer; I'll say that for you. But thank you all the same." Many years had passed since anyone had called her a young woman.

She looked down at the book. "No, I don't think I would like travel that far now." She blushed. "To tell you the truth, I've never been in an aeroplane before and I really don't think I want to try it at this stage."

"But you must have gone off on holiday when you were…"

"Younger?" Alice interrupted.

"I was going to say, growing up."

"I see." She looked away. "No, back then times were hard. We didn't have money for foreign holidays. Then when Dad was killed in an accident, Mum took a stroke. She was never the same again. I have spent most of my life looking after her. She relied on me totally. She only died last year." Alice fell silent. She hadn't meant to say so much.

"I see," said the gentleman. "What about your husband, wasn't he able to help you? By the way, my name is George Wilkes, I only moved into the area a few weeks ago.

"I'm Alice Harper and I've lived in this town all my life. I thought you must be a newcomer. I know most of the people in the town. And I'm not married; never had the opportunity to meet young men." She paused. "But I mustn't keep you. What book did you say you were looking for?" She made as if to stand up.

"Forget about the book, you're on your lunch break. I shouldn't have disturbed you." He pushed Alice's travel book back towards her. "I'll leave you to read in peace."

"I wasn't actually reading it. I feel rather restless today and I don't know why…" She broke off and suddenly thumped her fist on the table, making George jump. "Yes I do know. I'm bored with my life." Seeing George glance at the book she added. "Oh, I don't want to go off to the Caribbean, or anywhere fancy like that, but I would like to do something different. My life is as mundane as… as…" She glanced out of the window. "That number fifty seven bus outside."

George turned to look out of the window. Sure enough, there was a number fifty seven bus parked at the bus stop.

Alice burst out laughing. "You must think I'm crazy."

"No I don't. It's good for everyone to let off a little steam now and again." He paused. "But what I can't understand is, why the number fifty seven bus?"

"Because that poor old bus is the Town Service and spends all day and every day running around the town." She laughed. "It brings me here in the morning and then takes me home again in the evening. In between it does the same route over and over again. Like me it never gets a change. Never gets a chance to go anywhere different."

Alice looked away. "Now you *will* think I'm crazy."

"No I don't," said George slowly. "It's just never really thought of it like that before. But what gives you the idea that buses have the ability to understand what they are doing? They're only machines; made up from metal."

"That's true, but all these metal parts are put together by people," said Alice defiantly. She wished she hadn't got into this conversation, but now that she had, she was going to make a stand for the bus. "Surely, some of the thoughts, aspirations and frustrations of these people could have found the way into each small part as it was being created."

George looked interested. "I see what you're getting at – I think."

"Of course you do." Alice was on a roll and determined to make her point. "The happiness or sadness of people is transferred to other humans and animals and, according to gardeners, even plants. So why not machines, or the like?

"Well, I've got to say I've never thought of it like that before," said George.

"It certainly gives you something to think about doesn't it?" said Alice. "And if that bus could speak it would tell you that once in a while it would like to do something different."

"A bit like Chitty, Chitty, Bang, Bang?" asked George, grinning.

They looked at each other and burst out laughing.

"You really had me going there," said George. "For a moment I thought you were going to stand outside with a banner reading, 'Fair Deal for Buses'."

"Not all buses, just the number fifty seven," said Alice, grinning.

After that they got into deep conversation and the time simply flew by. It was only when the church clock chimed that Alice jumped to her feet. "My goodness is it that the time already?" Her lunch break had finished fifteen minutes ago. She hurried down to the front desk, where Anne was stamping a customer's book.

"You'd better get off home now. I'm sorry, but I completely forgot the time."

Once Anne had left, Alice offered to help George find the book he came in for.

"The book? Oh yes, the book. You know I'd almost forgotten about that. I want to look up my family tree and was wondering if there was something in the library to help with my research."

Alice went to a shelf and brought back a heavy old book. "I'm sure this one will get you started. Another customer was doing the same thing last year and I know he borrowed this one. He found it useful."

"Thank you, Alice. I must say I've enjoyed our little chat today. Perhaps you would let me take you out to lunch one day."

"That would be very nice George." She wanted to add, 'I shall look forward to it', but held back. He might not really mean it and besides, it wouldn't do to sound too eager.

Nevertheless Alice felt much brighter that afternoon and whether George took her to lunch or not, at least she had enjoyed his company for a short while. He had been a good listener.

That evening the number fifty seven bus came along on time just as it always did. She smiled to herself as she climbed on board. It was only through talking about the bus that she and George had got on so well.

But though Alice looked out for him over the next week, he didn't come into the library. She reminded herself that the book he had borrowed was very thick and would take a while to read. Nevertheless it would have been nice if he had popped in to let her know how he was getting on.

Today was her day off. If he went into the library this morning, she wouldn't be there. Was that what he was waiting for? Had he changed his mind about taking her to lunch? People often say things they later regret.

Usually her day off was spent cleaning around the house and doing her weekly shop. "My life is so predictable," she murmured as she stepped into the shower. "I could set a watch by my actions."

However, just as she was combing her hair, the sound of a vehicle pulling up outside caused her look out of the window. She rubbed her eyes in disbelief at the sight before her. For there, parked at front gate, was the number fifty seven bus. The driver honked his horn just as George stepped down onto the pavement.

Alice ran downstairs and out of the front door. "What on earth is going on?" she asked. "The bus stop is in the next street."

"I've come to take you out for the day," said George. "It occurred to me that your lunch break wouldn't be long enough for us to get to know each other properly, so I thought a day trip to the coast would be better." He turned towards the bus, his eyes twinkling. "And knowing how you feel about this bus, I thought you might like to take it with us. I've even hired the driver for the day. What do you think, Alice? Will you come?"

Laughing, Alice ran across to the bus and ran her fingers down the handle on the door. "It really is the old number fifty seven bus! I'd know it anywhere from the distinctive scratches under the handle. I think it's the craziest, but most wonderful thing anyone has ever done for me. How did you know it was my day off?"

"I made it my business to find out. Now, will you come?"

"Of course I'll come!" she replied, tears running down her cheeks. "You don't think I'd turn down the first exciting thing to happen to me in years, do you? I'll get my coat."

Alice couldn't remember ever having such a lovely day. George had pre-booked a table for lunch in one of the most prestigious hotels on the sea-front. Then after lunch, they walked along the beach to the lighthouse, talking and laughing like a couple of teenagers. She was most disappointed when darkness fell and it was time to board the bus and return home.

As the bus trundled along the country roads towards the town, George slipped his hand in hers. "I've so enjoyed your company Alice. I do hope you'll agree to let me take you out again."

"Of course I will. I've had wonderful day." She paused and laughed. "And I'm sure the bus has as well."

By the time the bus reached Alice's house, George had asked her out to dinner the following evening and was also talking about visiting the theatre another night.

She felt as though she was caught up in a whirlwind. Her life had taken a whole new turning and was going in a direction she had never thought possible, especially at her age.

Alice gave the bus a pat as it pulled away from the kerb. She blushed when she saw George watching her.

"I know it may seem silly to you, George," she said. "But I believe the number fifty-seven bus has played a large part in my newfound happiness."

He took her hand. "In our newfound happiness," he corrected her. "And I couldn't agree more."

Only the Best

"Why did I allow myself to be talked into this," I mumbled, as I laid out the agendas "I should have been more firm." But Mrs. Peterson had been so insistent.

"Of course you must be secretary, my dear," she'd said, her shrill voice piercing the silence of the church hall. "Your office skills make you perfect for the job. Our last one let me down very badly."

Though the previous secretary left to have a baby, Mrs. Peterson always maintained she had let the side down.

I had only been a member of the local amateur dramatic society for a short while, having recently moved into the area, but I'd quickly learned that Mrs. Peterson, the chair-lady, was accustomed to getting her own way.

I recalled our telephone conversation earlier, when she had asked me to add something to the agenda. "I'm afraid I won't have time to redo them," I'd told her. "I'll be at the office until well past six."

"How inconvenient, Sarah. Can't you retype them at the office? Surely the firm won't object when they hear how important it is."

"I'm not sure they..." I'd begun.

But Mrs. Peterson wasn't listening. "Thank you, my dear; I knew I could rely on you. See you tonight."

I sighed. Maud Peterson was full of her own importance. She believed herself to a great actress and director, but from what I'd seen, she had little talent for either. Though, on reflection, she could throw a tantrum at the drop of a hat.

Only a few weeks ago, she had caused a scene because her tea wasn't served in her own china cup and saucer. Jumping to his feet, Major Hadley had rushed to change it for her and was rewarded with a most gracious smile.

I hadn't understood why he fussed over her until Ted reminded me she would soon be choosing the roles for the next production. "I rather think he fancies himself as Professor Higgins," he'd said, with a knowing wink.

Placing a newly sharpened pencil by Mrs. Peterson's pad, a thought suddenly occurred to me. What if she saw herself as Eliza? It wouldn't be beyond the realms of possibility. I'd already heard how she had cast herself in the lead for their last production, 'Sweet Charity'.

Totally embarrassed; everyone had wondered how to tell her she was wrong for the role. But Ted, our lighting technician, bluntly told her, "You can't play the part of Charity. You have hips like a barn door and chins that wobble when you laugh."

But it was just like Ted to grab any opportunity to score points against her. He even called her Maud, occasionally, simply to annoy her, it being a name she was none too keen on.

The faint chiming of the church clock drew me back to the present. I knew the committee members would be punctual;

Mrs. Peterson frowned on latecomers, often reprimanding them like children.

I remembered Ted receiving the sharp edge of her tongue only recently, when he'd arrived a few minutes late. "It's so unprofessional, Ted." Taking his mumblings of sarcasm to be an apology, she'd accepted it, adding, "See it doesn't happen again."

"Pompous woman," he'd said to me over a cup of tea afterwards. "Why for two pins, I'd..." But the rest went unsaid, as he had almost choked when Major Hadley offered a vote of thanks for 'our wonderful chair-lady'.

"Crawler," he'd whispered, recovering his voice.

"Ah! Sarah." Mrs. Peterson's voice made me jump. "Tom won't be here tonight. It seems he was messing about up a ladder and fell off. He's broken his leg. How inconsiderate of the man. What was he doing up there?"

"He's a house painter, Mrs. Peterson. Where else would you expect him to be?" I had to agree, though, it was bad news. Tom, also a good carpenter, was our props man.

"Nevertheless, it was thoughtless of him to allow it to happen just as we're about to start our new production." Mrs. Peterson looked irritated. "However," she continued, brightening a little. "My own dear husband has kindly stepped in to save the day. Naturally Major Hadley volunteered to assist, as well as taking on the role of Professor Higgins. He's so thoughtful."

"I didn't think you were disclosing the roles until this evening."

"I haven't disclosed the roles, Sarah," she said haughtily. Last night the major kindly invited my husband and I to dine with him. I decided then to inform him of my decision."

"Good evening, my dear Major." Pushing me aside, Mrs. Peterson strode across the hall to greet him. "Punctual as ever, I see." Her voice floated back to me. "But then good manners and punctuality are something I've come to expect from someone of your breeding."

Once the whole committee had arrived, Mrs. Peterson declared the meeting open. Her smile rested on the major as she informed us of her decision to cast him as Professor Higgins. "Naturally being a military man, he has the bearing to carry it off well. Now I shall..."

"I disagree," interrupted Ted. "Major Hadley is too old."

"Professor Higgins is a distinguished, mature gentleman. I believe the major..." Mrs. Peterson began.

"The major's well past mature, Maud, he's old," Ted interrupted. He was determined not to be put off. "Eliza's a lovely young woman; she's not going to fall for an old codger like him. Who's playing Eliza by the way?"

Mrs. Peterson coughed.

Ted leapt to his feet. "Surely you're not thinking of playing the part yourself, Maud. Good heavens, woman, we'll be laughed off the stage. The part's made for someone young, not some..."

"Really Ted," the major protested. "I demand you apologise to Mrs. Peterson immediately."

Ted sat down. "I won't." He stubbornly folded his arms and looked the other away.

"If you had let me finish, Ted," said Mrs. Peterson. "I was about to say that Janet would make a good Eliza. Sarah will understudy her." She glanced at the major and smiled warmly. "With Ted's permission, I'll continue."

Ted remained silent as she read out the cast. "Now, if no one has any objections, my own dear husband, with some help from the major, will take over the scenery; Tom has foolishly broken his leg."

Ted opened his mouth to speak, but wishing to avoid another scene, I intervened. "Mrs. Peterson, my brother is visiting me shortly. He'll be staying for a few weeks. I'm sure he would be more than willing to advise us. He's…"

"My dear, Sarah," Mrs. Peterson broke in. "I know you mean well and I'm sure your brother is adequate at whatever it is he does. But I fear he would be out of his depth. Working with a society such as ours would be too much of a challenge for him."

"Yes, but…"

She held up her hand. "Naturally you must support your brother. However, I must point out that we have a high reputation in the community. They expect the very best from us. Therefore we can't lead them to believe we're a group of amateurs."

"But we are, aren't we?" Ted said looking her straight in the eye.

At which point, Mrs. Peterson shuffled her papers and declared the meeting closed.

"Ted, why do you torment her?" I asked on our way home.

"Well, someone should. Maud always gets her own way. No one stands up to her. Tell me, what other dramatic society would allow the chair-person to draw up the cast without any consultation?"

He had a point. At my last group, everything was properly debated. I couldn't understand why Mrs. Peterson had been allowed to have her own way for so long.

"And as for the scenery," Ted interrupted my thoughts. "I doubt your brother could make a worse job of it than those two. Did you hear about the shed Mr. P. put up?"

I shook my head. "Was it bad?"

"I'll say it was bad. Factory made, it was. There were four sides and an apex roof. Mr. P's brother came to help, but they still got it wrong. They hung the door before putting the sides together."

He laughed. "Mr. P. nailed the corners together from the inside while his brother supported it from the outside. Once it was finished, Mr. P. couldn't get out." Ted laughed even harder. "They'd only butted the side with the door next to the house wall. Maud was furious; she had to call the fire brigade to get him out."

When we reached my gate, he suddenly stopped laughing. "But now it's serious. She wants to let him loose on our stage sets." He shook his head "It's a bad business. Well, good night Sarah."

Rehearsals were soon underway. Ted had been right about the major. He wasn't really Professor Higgins material, though Mrs. Peterson didn't appear to notice.

But it was the props, which concerned me the most. It was obvious that neither Mr. Peterson nor the major could paint and, as for their woodwork, nothing would fit.

Again I tried offering my brother's services, but Mrs. Peterson brushed me aside. "No thank you, my dear. My husband and the major are doing splendidly. We're too good for amateurs, only the very best will do."

The first night arrived. Janet, having taken ill with stomach pains, left me to stand in for her.

Believing my look of concern was stage fright, Mrs. Peterson tried to assure me. "Don't worry, Sarah. Our own dear major will be by your side every step of the way."

However, my fears lay not with my part as Eliza, but with the stage scenery. If only Mr. P. and the major hadn't been so ambitious. Only last night, the freshly painted backdrop fell to the floor during a scene change when some new electronic gadget they had fitted, suddenly blew up. Oh my goodness, if that was to happen on our first night…

My thoughts were interrupted as the curtain rose. Major Hadley, taking one look at the audience, shrunk back into the wings.

"I can't go on." He wiped his hand across his forehead. "I'm ill, I feel faint."

"You must go on, major. Your public is waiting." Mrs. Peterson fanned him with a programme. "Besides, you can't let me down."

I peeked out at the audience. There was a slight hum of voices, they were growing restless. I knew the major's understudy was here, but he wasn't in costume.

"For heaven's sake, man, pull yourself together. Go out there and get on with it." No one had seen Ted leave his lighting control box.

"What!" The major jumped. "Eh, yes, Ted." He walked slowly onto the stage and stared out at the audience. It took another few minutes before he finally uttered his first line.

If that had been the only problem, we might have got away with it, but worse was to follow. During the show, several of the stage sets took on a life of their own. Cupboard doors refused to open and uneven shelves caused books and ornaments to slide off.

Instinctively the major, once a keen rugby player, dived to save a few before they reached the floor and crashed into a coffee table sending everything flying.

Then it was the turn of the door, centre stage. It stubbornly refused to budge. Characters were forced to make their exit by shuffling awkwardly towards the wings.

The major however, determined not to have his best scene ruined, heaved at the door with all the strength he could muster. Unfortunately, Mrs. Peterson chose that exact moment to try pushing it from the other side and suddenly found herself in a crumpled heap on the stage.

But it didn't end there. The large, unsecured tree outside the professor's window, which had wobbled dangerously throughout the entire performance, decided fall over and brought down the whole backdrop. Sparks flew as the electronic gadget bounced around the stage.

Finally, the shelving, having lost the will to stay up, crashed to the floor in a last-minute gesture of defiance.

Though the cast carried on bravely, the audience was helpless with laughter. "Best laugh I've had in years," said one lady. "Are there any tickets left for tomorrow night?"

Afterwards we all squeezed into the kitchen. The celebratory bottles of champagne stood unopened. Mrs. Peterson was inconsolable.

"Super show. You gave a really interesting new slant on Pygmalion." My brother grinned cheekily in the doorway.

"I've seen you somewhere before," said Ted.

"Mrs. Peterson looked up. "Yes. Don't you work in the D.I.Y shop?

"No…" my brother began.

"I know," interrupted Ted excitedly. "I saw you on TV."

"Yes Ted, you're right," I said, proudly. "He was receiving two awards for his stage set designs in West End theatres."

Mrs. Peterson looked at him and groaned.

Ted laughed. He was enjoying all this. "Yes, Maud. I can honestly see how a group like ours would be a challenge to him.

"Never mind, Mrs. Peterson, there's always tomorrow night and I'm sure my brother will help us out." Smiling broadly, I looked towards Mr. P. and the major. "Unless of course, you still believe that only the best will do."

The Suitcase

Lucy glanced at her watch and was surprised to find it was almost five o'clock. Sorting through her grandparents' cottage was proving to be more difficult than she had first thought. She was spending too long gazing at the various pieces of nostalgia Gran had kept down the years, but they brought back such happy memories.

Sadly, they had both died within a short space of time, leaving her mother unable to face clearing their home. Therefore Lucy, her husband Alan, and her elder sister Alice, had offered to do it. But then quite suddenly, Alice caught a rather nasty cold and Alan was called away on business, leaving Lucy to cope on her own.

Despite making a start on Friday evening after work, it was now late Saturday afternoon and she still hadn't finished downstairs. Nevertheless, she would have to leave soon. Alan would be arriving home shortly and she wanted to be there to greet him. Lucy was on the point of leaving for the day, when she felt a sudden urge to look in the cupboard under the stairs.

Peering inside, long forgotten memories flooded her mind. She remembered how Gran had always favoured her over Alice, often sharing a secret with her or hiding a small gift for her to find.

Lucy giggled. Gran had always used this very cupboard as a hiding place, mainly because Alice never ventured in here. Like their mother, Alice was terrified of the large, black spiders that lurked in the darkness. Strangely, Lucy had never had that problem.

She sighed, as she glanced around the cupboard. There wasn't much to see, how odd that she had felt the need to look in here. She was about to close the door, when she heard a rustling sound and moved forward to take a better look. It was then that she saw a battered suitcase poking out from between some newspapers. Brushing aside two spiders, she pulled out the case.

Looking closely, she saw that there were some initials on the lid. Though they had faded over the years, she could still make out the letters J.B. – Jane Beaumont, her grandmother's maiden name.

Lucy tried to open the case, but found it was locked. Obviously the case must hold a few items of jewellery that had been precious to Gran. However, she recalled finding several keys in an old vase that afternoon; it was possible that one of them might open it. Lucy decided to take the case home and look at the contents there.

Back home, she slipped a casserole into the oven to warm through, before attempting to open the case. Her fingers trembled as she tried each of the keys in turn, until at last the latch sprang open.

Inside there were bundles of letters and at the top was a picture of her grandparents on their wedding day. Lucy traced her fingers around the two figures in the photograph. Over the years, she had learned that since their marriage after the war ended, they had never once been apart.

Lucy pulled a bundle of letters from the case. The top one was addressed to Miss Jane Beaumont. Lucy's eyes filled with tears when she read how awful it had been for her grandfather to leave his beloved Jane, when he was shipped off to fight in France. Now he couldn't wait to see her again. It was such a lovely letter; it was little wonder that Gran had kept it all these years.

But as Lucy read the final sentence, she was shocked to see that the letter was not from Granddad at all. The signature was of someone called Albert. Grandfather's name was Edward!

The letter slipped through her fingers and dropped to the floor. Who on earth was Albert? Lucy had never heard his name mentioned before. Glancing at the other letters in the suitcase, she wondered whether there were any more from this man.

She poured herself a glass of wine, before picking up another envelope. This one was also addressed to Gran. Pulling out the letter she immediately looked for the signature. Again it was from Albert. However the following two letters in the bundle were from Granddad. Then she found a letter from her grand-mother addressed to Albert.

'My darling Albert,' it began. Lucy's eyes widened as she read the letter. Gran spoke of her love for him and how she hoped he would return home safely so they could be married as planned.

Lucy was horrified. How could her grandmother have strung two men along like that? The letters proved both men were in love with her and from the wording, it seemed that each one believed Gran was in love with him.

Disgusted, she threw the letters into the case and slammed the lid shut. This wasn't the grandmother she knew and loved. Her Gran was honest and decent. If only she hadn't found the wretched suitcase.

A beeping sound coming from the kitchen told her the meal was ready. She reset the oven to low. Alan shouldn't be long now and he would be hungry, though she had lost her appetite.

Back in the sitting room, she refilled her wine glass and switched on the television, hoping it would take her mind away from the letters. Yet her thoughts kept drifting back to the contents of the suitcase.

When Alan arrived home, Lucy wanted to tell him what she had found. However he looked so tired, she decided it could wait until morning.

"How did your day go?" Alan poured himself a glass of wine, as Lucy dished out the dinner.

"I'm afraid I didn't get very far," she said. "I spent too long reminiscing." She glanced across at the small case.

"What's in there?" he asked, following her gaze.

Lucy shrugged. "Nothing much. I'll tell you about it tomorrow."

However later, when they sat down to watch TV, her eyes kept straying across to the small case. In the end Alan insisted she told him what was bothering her.

"Oh Alan, it's awful," she wailed. "All my life I've looked up to Gran. She stood for everything that was good in life, but tonight I learned that she was two-timing Granddad during the war."

"Are you really sure about that?" Alan frowned.

"Of course I'm sure. The letters are in here." She handed him the suitcase. "And she even had the nerve to keep all their correspondence in the very house she shared with Granddad."

Lucy looked away. The thought of having to go back to the cottage haunted her, but she had to finish the job.

Alan broke the silence. "Did you read everything in here?"

"No," said Lucy. "But I read enough."

"Why don't we go through all the letters together?" Alan persisted. "There might be a reasonable explanation."

Lucy wasn't sure that she wanted to read anymore, however, after a reassuring nod from Alan, she pointed at the letters at the top. "That one is from Gran to Albert. She says she's looking forward to their wedding."

He read it quickly before handing it to Lucy. "What about all these others? Your grandmother must have written to your grandfather."

"I don't know. I didn't want to read any more after I saw Gran's letter to Albert."

Without a word, Alan picked up a few of the letters Lucy had read earlier.

"You'll see that both men say they are due some leave. It would have served Gran right if they'd both turned up on her doorstep at the same time," said Lucy, icily. "She would have had some explaining to do." She hesitated. "Come to think of it, I'm surprised that Gran has all the letters here."

Alan looked up. A question hung on his lips.

"What I mean is," continued Lucy. "I can understand her having the letters she sent to Granddad. He probably kept them until the war was over and brought them home. But how could she have the ones she wrote to Albert?" She paused. "Unless he returned them when he found she'd been two-timing him."

"Look, like I said, we'll go through them together. But you must realise it all happened a long time ago." Alan tried to calm her down.

"That's no excuse." Lucy didn't really feel like reading any more, however, Alan was already holding some letters towards her. Reluctantly, she reached out and took them from him.

The first one was much the same as the others she had read. Gran spoke of her love for Albert and how he was constantly in her thoughts. But then Lucy came to a letter addressed to Edward.

"Now then, Gran," Lucy mumbled. "Let's see what you wrote to poor Granddad." However, she was quite taken aback to find that her grandmother hadn't written words of love to Edward. Instead she told him about the local people and what they were doing. She even mentioned that Albert was coming home on leave very soon.

"I don't understand." Lucy handed the letter to her husband. "This is a letter to Granddad, but it's nothing like those she wrote to Albert."

Going through some of the other letters in the suitcase, they found that although Edward spoke of his love for Lucy's grandmother, she never once said she loved him.

"It seems your grandmother didn't love Edward after all," said Alan, still looking through the letters.

"If that's the case, then why did she marry him?" Lucy retorted. "Why lead Albert on if she was going to marry Edward in the end."

Alan didn't answer. He had found an official looking envelope in the suitcase. He held it out to Lucy. "Perhaps this will solve the mystery."

Lucy opened the letter. It was a brief message from the War Office, saying that the troop ship carrying Albert Armstrong home on leave had been sunk and he was missing, presumed drowned. They went on to say that he had left all his personal effects with a friend, requesting they be sent to her in the event of his death.

Tears filled Lucy's eyes as she sank back into her chair. The man Gran loved deeply had been killed, so that was why she had finally married Edward.

"Oh Alan, how sad for poor Gran," she sobbed. "But at least Granddad was there to comfort her and she found happiness with him. So that's the end of the story."

"Not quite." Alan was still rummaging through the case and had found two more letters. "There's more."

"No! That's it. The End," Lucy shrieked. "Albert was killed. Don't tell me there was another man in Gran's life."

"No, there wasn't anyone else." Alan paused and held up the two letters. "These are from Albert. They're both dated some months after the war had ended."

"But we know that he died." Lucy didn't feel she could take anymore.

"No. It seems he survived." Alan waved one letter in the air. "Here he tells your grandmother that he was picked up and taken prisoner and sent to a prisoner of war camp. He adds that only his love for her helped him through those dreadful days and now he's desperate to see her again." Alan looked away before continuing. "However the other one is his reply to a letter your Gran wrote, telling him of her marriage to Edward." He paused. "I think you'd better read it for yourself."

"I don't know that I want to," said Lucy. She was feeling ashamed at having so misjudged her grandmother. Yet she knew she must. Her fingers trembled as she took the letter from Alan.

"My darling Jane, please don't be sorry." Lucy read the words aloud. "I understand that believing I was dead, you had to make a new life for yourself. I agree that, though I shall never stop loving you, we can never see each other again." He ended by wishing both her and Edward much happiness in their life together.

Looking up from the letter, Lucy's eyes filled with tears. "That is so sad. Albert had survived the war, yet they could never be together."

"Could your mother and sister know about Albert?" asked Alan.

"No, I don't think so and I don't think Gran wanted them to know," said Lucy, slowly.

"Why not?" Alan looked puzzled. "After all, either one of them could have found the letters at any time."

Lucy didn't answer. She was reflecting on how she came to be the only one at the cottage today. Then there was her sudden urge to look in the cupboard and the strange rustling sound that led her to the suitcase. Was Gran behind it all? But Alan would say she was being fanciful.

"No they wouldn't," she said, at last.

"How can you be so sure?"

"Because Gran wanted *me* to find them and she wanted me to be alone at the time." Lucy paused. "She was sharing one last secret with me. She even hid the suitcase where she knew only I would find it."

"But you said it was in the cupboard under the stairs, surely Alice could just as easily have been the one to clear it out." Alan still didn't understand.

"Mum and Alice would never have gone into the cupboard under the stairs. That would have definitely been my job." Lucy laughed. "You see, Alan, there's always lots of big, black, hairy spiders in there and as you know, they're both terrified of spiders."

The Wrong Horse

Detective Inspector Keith Nichols chuckled to himself as he sank into his favourite chair. He was off duty for three weeks. Tomorrow he was flying to New York.

His wife, Sue was already out there. Unable to contain her excitement, she had caught the first available flight when their daughter had given birth ten days early. However, work commitment had forced him to wait until now.

He slapped his knee. He was a granddad. How about that? The officers at the police station had teased him mercilessly about it. But seriously, he was tickled pink and couldn't wait to see the boy.

A grandson! A tear spilled down onto his cheek. Already he could see presents for years ahead. Footballs, boxing gloves...

The telephone rang, interrupting his thoughts. Brushing away the tear, he picked up the receiver. "Inspector Nichols."

"Sorry to trouble you, sir." Sergeant Cook's voice came down the line. "But there's been a shooting at The Grange. I'm afraid the Major has committed suicide. Open and shut I'd say, but we need a senior officer at the scene."

"For heaven's sake. I'm off duty. I go on holiday tomorrow. Where's Inspector Peters?"

The sergeant coughed. "He called in sick. If you could just take a look, it should be straight-forward, being a suicide note and all. The pathologist has been informed. Dr. Andrews is on duty this evening. Between you, I'm sure you'll close the whole thing up tonight."

The inspector sighed. "Alright. But don't let anyone touch anything until I get there."

He put down the phone. It was always the same. Whenever he was going away, someone decided to do something stupid. Didn't people realise that policemen had lives too?

By the time he reached The Grange, the place was buzzing with newspaper reporters.

"I'm glad you could come, sir." The sergeant stepped aside to allow the inspector to pass.

"Who found the body?" Inspector Nichols pushed past a photographer.

"His wife, sir," replied the sergeant. "She came home to find Major Alderson dead in his study. I imagine it was quite a shock for the poor woman. A WPC is with her now."

He paused, looking down at his notes. "She'd been to a charity event. The butler and the maid were also out."

"Isn't that strange; the butler and the maid both being out on the same evening?" Inspector Nichols raised his eyebrows.

The sergeant nodded. "Yes I thought that, but apparently they're a married couple and had been invited to the evening reception of a wedding. As the house wouldn't be empty, what with the major being at home, Mrs. Alderson saw no reason to object."

It had been raining heavily and the two policemen wiped their feet before stepping onto the thick pile carpet in the hall.

"In there, sir." The sergeant pointed towards the study.

Inspector Nichols stood in the doorway and looked at the scene. From his position he could see the major's body slumped over the desk. He noted that the safe, located on the major's left, was wide open.

"Has anyone touched anything?"

"No," replied the sergeant. "Mrs. Alderson told me she used the phone in the hall to contact the police. The pathologist and his team haven't arrived yet."

Nodding thoughtfully, Inspector Nichols walked across to the desk, pausing only to inspect some mud on the carpet.

"Probably from Mrs. Alderson's shoes," the sergeant volunteered.

"Perhaps," murmured Nichols, moving towards the desk.

Without touching the major's body, he carefully checked the gun wound to the head. Then he turned his attention to the desk.

An old army revolver was resting in the major's right hand, while a pen, presumably the one used to write the note, lay a little towards the left of the blotter. The slightly crumpled suicide note was at the front of the desk.

Twisting his neck a little, the inspector read the words. 'I backed the wrong horse!' Looking closely, he saw that the top edge of the paper was slightly ragged.

"Could have been caused when the sheet was pulled from the pad?" suggested the sergeant, following the inspector's gaze.

"Yes, indeed," the inspector mumbled, without looking up.

He noted that the Major seemed to be a very tidy man. The centre of his desk was clear. The pens, all but the one used to write the note lay neatly in a tray. Paper clips and other items of stationery were all in their appropriate containers. On the left were several framed photographs. With the exception of one, they were lined up like soldiers on parade.

Taking a closer look, the inspector found that the offending photograph showed the major with two men. They were standing by some horses in the paddock at a racecourse.

"Just like I said; it's a clear case of suicide. The major gambled on a horse and lost. Probably couldn't face the wife." Sergeant Cook sounded triumphant.

"Could be." The inspector straightened up. After a final glance at the desk, he strode across to the safe.

"Was the safe door open when Mrs. Alderson found the body?"

"Yes. She thought it strange. Her husband usually kept it locked. But surely if he had lost his money on a horse, there wouldn't be anything in there."

Hearing a sound in the hall, the sergeant looked towards the door. "Dr. Andrews has arrived, sir. Will I show him in?"

"Yes. I've finished here for the moment. I'd like to speak to Mrs. Alderson."

The inspector nodded to the doctor; he was an old friend.

"I didn't expect to find you here, Keith." Ron grinned. "I thought you'd be on your way to see your new grandson."

"I fly out tomorrow." The inspector nodded towards the body. "Tell me what you can about the wound when you have looked at the Major's body."

Inspector Nichols found Mrs. Alderson in the drawing room.

"I'm sorry to trouble you at this time," he said, gently. "But I really need to ask you a few questions."

She sighed. "I understand."

The inspector nodded. "When you arrived home, did you remove your shoes before or after you went into the study?"

"Before!" Mrs. Alderson answered without hesitation. "It was raining; my shoes were muddy. We're waiting for a fresh delivery of gravel for the drive." She paused. "Is that important?"

"It could be," said the inspector, thoughtfully. "Was your husband a gambling man? I'm referring to the note on the desk."

"No. Not in the sense you mean," said Mrs. Alderson. "He enjoyed going to the races; the excitement of having the occasional flutter. But he would never gamble £4000 on a horse. That's the amount missing from the safe."

"Oh don't worry!" she added, quickly. "I didn't touch it; I've seen enough TV dramas to know not to touch anything at the scene of a police investigation."

The inspector hid a smile as Mrs. Alderson continued.

"The door was wide open; I could see at a glance that the money was gone. I was present last night when my husband put it there. It was piled neatly on the left hand side of the top shelf. Being left-handed, he placed anything of any importance on his left."

She paused. "My husband was a very precise man. He liked everything to be tidy. If something was out of line, he would straighten it. Comes from all those years in the army, I suppose."

"Yes," said the inspector, slowly. He thought back to the desk in the study. "The photograph on your husband's desk, the one where he's standing next to two men, would you tell me who the men are?"

"Charles Rigby and David Sanders," said Mrs. Alderson. "They served with my husband in the army. Michael invited them to join the business when they were discharged. Not having a family of our own, he decided to groom one of them to take over when he retired. Both men were first class; my husband found it a difficult choice. But finally, he chose Charles and consulted our solicitor, an old family friend, to draw up a contract."

She looked up quickly. "Charles! Oh my goodness, I should have telephoned to let him know. He won't believe it; my husband was talking to him on the phone earlier this evening."

"We'll see to it," said the inspector, nodding to the WPC.

"His number is in the book by the phone," said Mrs. Alderson.

"You said they spoke this evening." Inspector Nichols turned back to Mrs. Alderson. "Did you hear what your husband said?"

"No. I'm sorry. I just heard him call Charles by name as I left." Mrs. Alderson shook her head in dismay. "I'm not much help, am I?"

"But you are," the inspector assured her. "It's a very difficult time for you." He hesitated. "Is David Sanders still with the business?"

"Yes, he is. Personally, I favoured him over Charles, but my husband thought otherwise." She paused. "Though lately, I wondered if he was having doubts."

"Did he say as much?"

"No." Mrs. Alderson shook her head. "Perhaps I was mistaken."

"How many people knew where your husband kept his gun?"

"Not many, only the butler, the maid, Charles and David" Mrs. Alderson counted on her fingers, "plus myself of course."

A commotion in the hall caused the inspector to look up. "What is it?"

"It's Charles Rigby, sir," said the WPC.

Pushing his way past Sergeant Cook, Charles burst into the room.

"I came to see the major, but…" Seeing Mrs. Alderson, he rushed to her side. "My dear, what can I say? I heard the news outside. How dreadful. I can't believe it."

He looked at the inspector. "I heard it was suicide."

"So did I." Inspector Nichols glanced at Charles' shoes. "But I'm not so sure."

"There's a note; what else could it be?" said Charles, hotly.

Inspector Nichols shrugged. "We shall see."

"May I speak to you for a moment, Inspector?" The voice came from Dr. Andrews.

Making his excuses, the inspector joined the pathologist in the hall.

"Obviously, the Major died of a gunshot wound to the head," said Dr. Andrews. "However, I'm not sure it was he who fired the gun. There's no doubt the gun was fired at close range, but

I can't say for certain who pulled the trigger. It could have been someone standing close by. I can't be more definite until I examine the body back at the mortuary."

"You've told me enough." The inspector went back into the drawing room.

"Mrs. Alderson, I have reason to believe that your husband was murdered."

"Murdered? Who would want to murder Michael?" Mrs. Alderson sounded shocked.

"Don't be ridiculous," said Charles angrily. "As Mrs. Alderson says, who would want to kill Michael?"

"You might," said the inspector, calmly. "I believe Major Alderson telephoned you this evening, informing you that he'd changed his mind and was going to make David his heir. You came here to speak to him in person hoping to change his mind."

The inspector pointed to Charles' muddy shoes. "You left a mud print on the carpet. However, the major refused to listen, so you took his revolver from the drawer and shot him. Too late, the Major realised what was happening. But, before you pulled the trigger, he knocked the photograph of you and David out of line. Normally so neat in his habits, he hoped someone would notice. Panicking, you placed the gun in the major's right hand – forgetting he was left handed."

"You're wrong," wailed Charles. "You saw the note; it was suicide."

"Ah yes; the note." Inspector Nichols smiled. "You saw his unfinished letter as a way out. Tearing off the name at the top, you hoped it would look like suicide. You even took the money from the safe, to make it more convincing. However, I believe the major was writing to his solicitor – another racing fan, I'll wager – informing him he had backed the wrong horse." He paused. "You see, Mr. Rigby, in racing circles, the phrase, 'to back the wrong horse', means you've made an error of judgement."

Reaching the Top

"How much further?" I puffed. "Surely we must be nearly there."

"I don't think there's far to go now." James' reassuring voice echoed from somewhere up ahead.

Pausing to catch my breath, I recalled the notice at the entrance of the tower. Three hundred and twenty five steps! I must be mad. At my age, I should have more sense than to attempt to climb to the top of the Cathedral Tower.

And to think I actually paid good money for this! Why, at this very moment, I could be sitting outside the local pub, raising a glass of gin and tonic to all those foolhardy enough to climb the tower steps.

"Are you alright?" James interrupted my thoughts. There was a note of concern in his voice. "We could always turn back if you're unsure."

Not likely! This was a challenge and having come this far, I wasn't about to give up now. I sighed, suddenly remembering how I had turned down a whole series of challenges over the last few months. What was so important about this one? Why was I punishing myself like this? And, come to think of it, what did I mean, 'at my age'? I wasn't that old – just a little unfit! I clenched my lips together. Alright! On reflection, a lot unfit – but who's counting?

"Ellen! Answer me! Are you alright?" The note of concern in James' voice had changed to one of urgency. "I'm coming down!"

"No! I'm fine." I called out. I tried to sound matter of fact. I didn't want him to hear me wheezing. "I'm just taking a breather. You carry on; once I get my second wind, I'll catch up and race you to the top."

I grimaced. I knew that was never going to happen. Apart from there being hardly any room to pass anyone on these narrow spiral stairs, I was in no state to race anyone anywhere. James probably knew it too. But I guessed he was too much of a gentleman to say so.

I shook my head, how could I even pretend to guess what James was like? In actual fact, I didn't know him at all. This outing had been organised by a group I had joined recently. James was our regional representative and I had only met him very briefly once before. Still, he seemed like a nice sort of a guy.

Today was supposed to be a fun day out; a sort of hand-shake event with members from a fellow organization in the next county. So far it had worked well; everyone was keen to make new friends. Together, James and Raymond, the other representative, had planned the whole thing. Though truthfully, this climb to the top of the tower hadn't been on their agenda. That rather foolish idea had been mine alone.

I recalled the next stop was lunch in the Cathedral café, after which, we were all going on a boat trip down the river. Now that was something I was looking forward to. I could already see myself lounging back in my seat, listening to the water as it rippled past the boat. I glanced up the stone steps and frowned. But first I had to get to the top of these wretched stairs.

Taking a deep breath, I forced my legs to move on, only to find I had to stop again as another group of people were coming down. This was the most terrifying part of the whole experience. There was hardly room for one person on the stairs, yet people already having been to the top, were making their way down.

"You still have some way to go," the first one told me, jovially.

Giving him a sickly smile, I gripped the metal handrail and pushed myself against the cold, stone wall, while he and about half a dozen others very gingerly squeezed past. Obviously when building the tower, the monks hadn't thought of making another staircase for those wishing to go down.

But back then, how many would have wanted to climb up here anyway? They probably had more sense than to drag themselves up all these stairs on a regular basis. Only those serving a penance would have been forced to climb up here to check that the roof and parapet were in good repair.

Then, just as a lady struggled to heave her rather large frame around me, I had another thought. Very shortly I would have to go through the whole procedure again on the way down. Only this time, those coming up would be holding the rail and it would be my turn to balance myself on the narrower edge of the steps.

I felt my heart do a kind of somersault and I swallowed hard. It was no good; I couldn't do it. Once I got to the top, I would have to stay up there until the man at the bottom called 'time' and realised there was still one person missing. He and his colleagues would then have to figure out a suitable way of getting me down.

But how would he know I was up there? Then I remembered he was using an abacus; checking people off as they went up and came down. Yet what if he was distracted and forgot to slide one of the beads along the row? Even worse, someone playing a joke might turn the thing around and throw his whole system into confusion. I wiped my brow; now I was letting my imagination run away with me. Of course James would tell them of my predicament.

I began to climb the steps again. Round and round they went. Would they never come to an end? How much more could my poor legs take? I paused to take another breather.

"I can see daylight," James called down, joyously.

"Good for you!" I murmured, slumping onto the stone steps. If this had been a bus, I could have rung the bell and jumped off long ago. No one would have noticed; it happened all the time. None of the other passengers knew how far anyone was travelling. But here it was different; there was only one stop, so to speak. Everyone would know I was admitting defeat.

Yet something nagged at me. If I really wanted go back, I would have done so before coming this far. For some reason, getting to the top had become an obsession.

"Did you hear?" James tried again. "I said I could see daylight."

"Great news," I called out still slumped on the stairs, I tried to sound enthusiastic for his sake. After all this wasn't James' fault. He had simply volunteered to accompany me. "Keep going. I'm right behind you," I quipped.

I couldn't really get excited; the light he mentioned was probably from a tiny slit, which served as a window in the tower wall. We had come across a one or two of those on the way up. Nevertheless, I suppose I could take another look to see how far I had come. The down side being I would also see how much further I had to climb.

"I was right! We've made it!" James exclaimed, his voice echoed down the winding staircase.

Who is this 'we'? I wondered. You've made it, James I'm still sitting here wondering if I will ever touch the ground again.

"Come on, Ellen. The views up here are spectacular; you can see for miles."

"I'm coming," I called out, stumbling to my feet. I still didn't know how much further I had to go. James' voice was muffled, making it difficult to tell how far ahead he was.

Making my way up the steps again, my legs turned to jelly; urging me to stop and give in. Yet I carried on, slowly placing one foot after another, until mercifully I saw the sunlight streaming through the small door leading to the roof of the tower. Almost crying with relief, I crawled on all fours up the remaining steps and tumbled through the doorway into the sunshine.

"Why did I let you talk me into this, James?" I uttered, staring up at his bewildered face.

Waving away offers of help, it took me a few moments to regain my dignity. But looking out across the parapet, I was so lost in admiration, all my embarrassment and tiredness drained away.

The views were stunning. Being such a clear day, I was able to make out landmarks I knew to be several miles away. Below the tower, sprawled the town. From here the shops and houses looked so tiny; reminding me of children's building blocks. Beyond the winding river, trees and fields in differing shades of green, stretched out like a huge luxurious carpet.

Tears filled my eyes as I gazed out across the scene. I had been so dreadfully wrong. It wouldn't have been a penance for those monks to come up here at all. They would have rejoiced at being given the chance to see so wondrous a sight.

The tears continued to roll down my cheeks, but now they weren't for the monks. They were for me. Only now did I realise why reaching the top had been so important.

A few months ago Paul, my husband, had left me for a younger model; a rather flashy blonde. I had been devastated. After all we had meant to each other, how could he have rejected me so cruelly?

Catching a glimpse of her in his car one day, I wondered what such a vibrant young woman could possibly see in Paul. She looked the sort who liked to party; a jet-setter.

But Paul wasn't like that at all. The Paul I knew was a plodder; never having been one for the night-life. So why was she so attracted to him? Then one day a couple of weeks or so after he had left me, I found him in my house looking for money.

Naturally I sent him packing and immediately set about changing the locks on the doors. But now I knew what she was after. Having seen Paul's expensive sports car and the house he lived in, his new girlfriend believed she had hit the jackpot! Well if that was the case, the lady was in for a big surprise. The money belonged to me. It had been left to me by a maiden aunt, and neither of them was getting a penny.

Nevertheless, terribly upset at being tossed aside, I had thrown myself into a fit of despair. Locking myself away, I only left the house when absolutely necessary. So concerned, my friends had invited me to various functions. I knew they meant well, but I had declined their invitations, fearing I would be pointed out as the wife whose husband had forsaken her.

Then one day, quite out of the blue, I saw an advertisement for a newly formed organization. They were looking for members. On the spur of the moment, I obtained an application form and posted it off; not allowing myself the time to change my mind. At least no one would know me and I didn't need to explain my failings. As far as the group was concerned, I had never even been married.

Marvelling the view from the tower roof, I knew now why I had been so determined to complete the challenge. Reaching the top of the tower was my way of hauling myself from the deep pit I had fallen into. And by Jove, it had worked. But also something else had happened. I felt my life had taken on a whole new meaning.

I now realised I wasn't a failure at all. I was alive and well and the big wide world out there was waiting for me. Paul had found someone else – so what? If that's what he wanted, she was welcome to him.

Yet at the same time one small part of me felt a little sorry for him. I had a feeling that once she found the money had dried up, his new romance wouldn't last. It would be his turn to feel the pain of rejection. Perhaps he would find a challenge of his own. But if he did, would he even take it on, let alone conquer it?

"Are you alright?" Looking anxious, James was shaking my arm. "I've been talking to you, but you seem miles away."

"Yes. I'm fine, James." I smiled. "Really I am." I paused. "To tell you the truth, I've never felt better. Reaching the top has turned my life around."

A puzzled expression appeared on his face.

"Don't you worry yourself about it," I said. I held up my camera. "I'll just take a few photos for my album and then we'll tackle those stairs again. All that climbing has made me feel quite hungry. What about you?"

Drastic Measures

I read the letter with dismay. Whether I liked it or not, it appeared I was now an official contestant in the local scone-making competition.

Recently married, Rob and I had moved into an idyllic cottage in the country. The villagers were very friendly and everything was wonderful – until our neighbour, the formidable Jane Bloomsbury, returned from holiday.

Believing married women should stay at home, she grabbed every opportunity to make me feel guilty about my role as a working wife. "A man needs his wife at home," was her most favourite saying.

I recalled how a couple of weeks ago she had been waiting for me coming home from the office. Fully expecting another lecture on domesticity, I had been surprised when she informed me of the local scone-making contest.

"It's a big event. Scones and pastry are considered an art in these parts; it's a matter of a good recipe and a light touch. Naturally I am an excellent pastry-cook; my scones are renowned." She had boasted. "But then, my recipes come from my grandmother, a lady who knew a thing or two about baking."

"Mrs. Bloomsbury," I'd said, foolishly falling into her trap. "I'm sure my pastry and scones are as good…"

"Put it to the test," she'd interrupted with a look of triumph. "Enter the competition."

"This is silly…" I began.

"You're afraid," she interrupted again. "You know you'll lose."

When I hotly disagreed, she handed me an application form, which just happened to be in her apron pocket. "I insist you fill it in. But as the closing date is this week, I'll post it for you." She smiled smugly. "I know how busy you working wives are."

Looking back now, I should have…

Rob's tread on the stair interrupted my thoughts.

"What's that, Lucy? Not another bill."

"No! It's worse." I showed him the letter.

He laughed. "Your scones aren't your best feature; from all accounts Mrs. Bloomsbury's melt in the mouth."

"Thank you for your support, Rob." Feeling hurt, I turned and walked towards the kitchen; he quickly followed.

"I'm sorry, Darling, I didn't mean… Your scones aren't all that bad. Besides, Mrs. B. doesn't have your other, more endearing qualities. Look, forget the wretched competition; tell her we have to go away on business. We'll go off somewhere; just the two of us. They're only scones, for goodness sake."

"If only Jane Bloomsbury saw it like that." I sighed. "Scones and pastry are her whole life."

"She needs to get out more!" Rob retorted.

We both laughed. "Going away is a lovely idea, Rob. But no! I must see this through."

"Well, if you're really sure." He grinned. "I suppose this means I'll be eating scones 'til they come out of my ears." Mimicking Mrs. Bloomsbury, he added. "Young wives today have no idea how to feed a healthy, red-blooded…"

The rest was lost as he deftly avoided the cushion I threw at him. Nevertheless, he was right; scones were not my best feature. Drastic measures were needed, but what could I do?

Later that morning at the office, my friends laughed at the list of rules involved in the competition; especially the one about a screen being placed between the contestants.

"It sounds more like an execution to me," said one.

"Scone and pastry-making is taken very seriously," I told her. "Recipes are handed down from their grandmothers."

Arriving home that evening, I found Mrs. Bloomsbury waiting for me.

"Yoo-hoo," her voice rang out. "I say, Lucy. Can you hear me?"

It was likely the whole street had heard her. "Yes, what is it?" I asked, wearily.

"Did you receive your acceptance letter this morning? I have mine here."

"Yes," I assured her. "It came today. But I must go, Rob will be home soon."

"You'll need a good recipe."

I tried not to laugh as her small piggy-like eyes darted back and forth as she spoke. "Yes and I have a very good one. But I haven't time to discuss it with you." I hurried indoors. That little act of bravado had got me nowhere. Now I was forced to come up with some superb scones.

That evening, I baked a batch. Keeping watch by the glass door of the oven, I almost did a jig around the kitchen when I saw them all rise beautifully. Perhaps scone-making wasn't so difficult after all. But suddenly, they keeled over, taking on a rocklike appearance.

Rob bravely chomped his way through one and then another, saying they were delicious. But I knew he was being kind and stopped him from taking a third. Dentist's bills were too expensive.

"It won't be long now. I'm so looking forward to the scone-making contest," Mrs. Bloomsbury said to me one evening in the village hall, she was the quiz-master that night. Her voice was so loud, everyone could hear.

Knowing she had everyone's attention, she carried on; her voice ringing across the hall. "This will be my tenth year of winning the trophy and…"

"How do you know you're going to win, Jane?" Moira interrupted. "Someone might beat you this year."

"Who?" Jane looked around the room. "Not you, Moira, dear, or any of you, come to that. You've all tried before. And as for Lucy…" She brushed me aside with a gesture of her hand. "She has no chance. It's only at my insistence she entered the contest at all. No! I'll win again and you all know it. I'll probably win the pastry contest again as well."

She turned back to me. "It's such a wonderful experience being presented with the trophy. My dear husband is so proud of me. Over the years he has learned I have something, which can't be suppressed. What I have is…"

"A big mouth!" Moira interrupted. She looked around the hall as laughter broke out.

"A talent!" Jane yelled, giving Moira an icy glare. "Quiet! I insist you all stop laughing immediately. We'll begin the quiz."

"I was right the first time," whispered Moira.

Back home I was upset. "I'm going to fail miserably."

"One of these days, she's going to open her mouth and put her foot in it." Rob tried to comfort me. "And Moira is right; there'd be plenty of room for it in there. Perhaps this year her scones will simply form a large blob in the oven."

I laughed. "I wish! If only I could come up with some scones that didn't emerge from the oven like rocks." I paused, suddenly thinking of my grandmother. Why hadn't I thought about her before?

She was always making scones for Granddad. Even his friends from the allotment were very partial to Gran's scones. It must take a darn good scone to satisfy the likes of that lot. I decided to call on her after work the following day.

Gran greeted me warmly and over tea in the garden, I told her about the local scone making competition. "My neighbour's an old busy-body who's trying to make me look foolish. She's insisted..." I paused, deciding to get straight to the point. "Gran, I know how much Granddad and his friends enjoy your scones. Would you give me your recipe?"

I held my breath. Even if she agreed, would her recipe be different to those I had tried already?

Gran laughed. "Who's judging the competition?"

"The local magistrate and the vicar," I answered. "But what's that got to do with it?"

Gran, still laughing, shook her head. "No. What I really mean is, are they men? You can't tell these days. Now when I was a girl…"

"Yes, they're both men," I interrupted. Once she began talking about her girlhood, there was no stopping her.

"Good. Half the battle's over already." She gave me a furtive smile. "But you must promise never to disclose it to anyone outside the family."

I gave my solemn promise, but my heart sank as I wrote down the list of ingredients. So far there was nothing different to the recipes I'd already tested.

"And now, Lucy, this is my very old, secret ingredient, it's what turns an ordinary fruit scone into a pure work of art."

My heart plummeted to my shoes. If this ingredient was so old, it was most unlikely I'd find it on the shelves in the modern supermarkets of today. There was no time to search out the shops of yesteryear; the competition was the next day.

Glancing from side to side, Gran made sure no one was in earshot. Instinctively, I did the same. I was beginning to feel like an MI5 spy. And all for a plate of scones!

Satisfied no one was listening, Gran leant forward and so did I. As she whispered the special, secret ingredient in my ear, a smile formed on my lips. This was something I could buy anywhere. In fact, there was some at home.

Gran went on to explain how this 'special' ingredient should be added to give the maximum effect.

The next morning I weighed out the ingredients exactly as Gran had instructed; except for two. Carefully following her instructions, I had already prepared those the evening before.

The village hall was full when I arrived and Mrs. Bloomsbury was already at her table. No one attempted to unpack their ingredients until the screens were in place.

Glancing at Mrs. Bloomsbury, I wished her luck.

"My scones don't need luck," she gloated. "They're winners."

Rob gave me a hug. "Don't worry about her, Just do your best."

I still hadn't told him of my visit to Gran.

At last the competition was underway. I followed Gran's instructions carefully, though she had said not to worry until placing the scones in the oven. "The timing is very important. Never, never overcook them, else all will be lost," her words still rang in my ears.

All too soon the tasting began. Looking at my scones sitting there on the plate, I felt anxious; the fruit had sunk to the bottom. But I reminded myself that Gran had said it would.

Mrs. Bloomsbury laughed as she looked down the line of contestants. "You have little chance of winning with those, Lucy. They must be like lead."

I held my breath as the judges came closer. The vicar, leading the way, was first to sample my scones. However instead of moving on, he lingered and took another. By now the magistrate had caught up with him.

"Move along there, Vicar," he said, taking one of my scones. After one mouthful, he looked first at the vicar and then at me. Devouring it quickly, he ran his tongue around his lips before picking up another.

Jane Bloomsbury watched closely as both judges kept returning back down the line to my plate of scones. Her face was a picture when they jostled each other for the last one.

At last it was time to announce the winner. "Without any doubt at all, we declare this year's winner to be Lucy Hadley," said the vicar.

Rob ran across to the table, "You did it, darling." He punched the air with delight.

Holding the trophy aloft, I looked across at Mrs. Bloomsbury. "You're absolutely right Mrs. B. It is the most wonderful feeling to be presented with the trophy. And it's all down to you; it was only at your insistence I even entered the contest at all. I really must do it again next year."

"You shouldn't have won at all." Mrs. Bloomsbury sounded almost hysterical. "Your scones didn't rise, there was far too much fruit in them and it all sank to the bottom. They weren't even in the oven long enough..."

"But the taste was outstanding," interrupted the magistrate. "Wouldn't you agree, vicar?"

"Without a doubt! Absolutely outstanding."

"Where would *you* get such an 'outstanding' recipe?" asked Mrs. Bloomsbury, trying to compose herself.

"Well," I said, enjoying myself. "It turns out I also have a grandmother who enjoys baking. Scones are her speciality, but her pastry is equally superb. I could very easily be persuaded to enter the pastry competition."

Mrs. Bloomsbury groaned.

"It's not been much of a day for you, Jane, has it?" Moira laughed. "Well done, Lucy. I don't know how you did it, but you've knocked the wind out of her sails right enough."

When Mrs. Bloomsbury stomped off, Rob turned to me. "How did you do it, Lucy? I promise not to tell anyone." As he spoke, he absentmindedly picked up the one, single, plump sultana left on my plate and popped it into his mouth.

I grinned at the expression of delight that suddenly spread across his face. The sultana, having exploded, had filled his mouth with the overwhelming tang of his most expensive brandy.

"You didn't?" he asked, grinning broadly.

"Oh yes I did," I whispered, nodding excitedly. I explained how more than treble the normal amount of sultanas had spent the night happily basking in half a litre of his very best Napoleon Brandy.

"Though Gran did say a small cupful of cheap brandy would suffice, I felt this was an emergency and needed more, shall we say, drastic measures."

To Trap a Thief!

I wonder if someone will try to steal it," whispered Helen. She and Marion were viewing a large jewel on loan to the museum from a rich gentleman. "It doesn't look very well guarded. I could almost reach out and touch it."

It was true. The jewel was mounted on an open display stand in a large, windowless room.

"You would get a shock if you did."

Helen and Marion jumped. Neither had heard the security man creeping up behind them.

"You idiot!" Helen exclaimed. "You could give someone a heart attack sneaking up like that." She paused. "What do you mean – get a shock? Is it wired to the national grid?"

He laughed. "No! Of course not! But touching it would interrupt a series of electronic beams, causing all sorts of things to happen." He pointed down to a metal strip running around the display stand. "See that? It's the rim of a strong steel cage, which would shoot out of the floor and trap the thief." He snapped his fingers. "Just like that!"

Drawing himself up to his full height, he gestured towards the corridor. "And that's not all. Shutters, cunningly hidden from view, would crash to the floor totally sealing off not only this room, but the entire building."

Now seemingly on a roll, he threw his arms into the air. "At the same time, sirens would blast throughout the museum and a separate link would alert the police station. And it's all done through modern technology; namely electricity. Nothing can go wrong."

"I see." Marion peered at the name tag pinned to his uniform. "So, Albert, everything is done through electricity."

"Absolutely!" Albert folded his arms proudly.

"Then what if there's a power cut?"

"I... err," blustered Albert, momentarily lost for words. "I must get on. As Chief of Security, I've more important things to do than to stand here gossiping."

However, on the point of moving away, he hesitated. "But even if anyone was able to bypass my security, they'd find their hands covered in a deep purple dye. The stone has been treated with a special solution." He smiled smugly. "Anyway, in answer to your earlier question, if there was a power cut, the museum's own emergency power would swing into action. As I said, the whole thing is foolproof."

"If the shutters seal off the building, how will the police get in?" Marion grinned.

"Naturally we'll open them once they arrive," retorted Albert.

"All this security must have cost a tidy sum," said Helen, thoughtfully.

"Too right it did." Albert smoothed down his jacket. "But this stone is worth the extra security; why it's safer here than in the Bank of England. No one can steal this jewel while it's under my protection." He rose up and down on the balls of his feet. "It was I who designed these security arrangements. I'm not without experience in such matters. The owner of the jewel himself approved my precautions."

"Incidentally, where is the owner?" Helen asked.

"He's on holiday and offered to lend us the jewel while he was away," Albert swaggered. Very generous, I'd say."

"Very crafty, more like," laughed Helen.

"What do you mean?" snapped Albert.

Helen shrugged. "Well look at it this way. The museum has gone to a great deal of expense to install all this equipment."

"So! What about it?" said Albert.

"Surely you must see," explained Helen, patiently. This guy is jet-setting around the world with his pals, safe in the knowledge that his jewel is being closely guarded by the museum. Yet the whole thing isn't costing him a single penny."

"And, if I remember rightly," chirped Marion. "The museum is paying him a cool £100,000 for the privilege of putting it on show, which means you're also paying for his holiday!"

"Exactly!" Helen looked at Albert. "This guy has taken the museum for a ride."

"You don't know what you're talking about!" exclaimed Albert, angrily. "Women have no idea how business works. Let me explain it to you. Firstly, there's an extra charge for people wishing to view the jewel." His eyes narrowed. "But perhaps you didn't pay the full amount at the entrance."

"Of course we did!" Helen was indignant. "We came especially to see the stone."

"Precisely! That was going to be my second point!" retorted Albert. "People will flock here to see this display. The extra revenue will pay for the security."

"I still think the jewel could be stolen," said Helen, tracing her foot along the metal strip on the floor. "And should someone by-pass your fancy security, the dye wouldn't show if the thief wore gloves."

"Gloves aren't allowed in this area," Albert sneered, pointing to a notice on the wall. "And before you make any more silly comments, our surveillance cameras would soon catch anyone removing gloves from their pocket." He sounded triumphant. "Not even I could take the stone out of the museum unnoticed!"

"I still believe someone could steal the jewel," mused Helen. By now, she and Marion were sitting in the coffee shop opposite the museum.

"You shouldn't let Albert get to you," Marion declared.

"I know. But he was so pompous; he wouldn't even listen to my concerns." Helen slammed her fist down on the table. "It would serve him right if someone took the wretched stone. Oh! I don't mean it should really be stolen," she added, hastily. "But wouldn't it be good to see Albert taken down a peg or two?"

Later that week the two ladies returned to the museum with their friend Gina.

"Come on, Helen!" Gina called out. She and Marion had gone on ahead; Helen lingered in the corridor.

"I would love to be the owner of something so precious." Gina gazed longingly at the jewel.

"What's the point? You'd always be afraid it might be stolen." Helen strode across the room. "Anyway, what do you think about the security?"

Gina gazed around. "It certainly looks easy to steal. However, both the museum and their insurance company are happy with the arrangements, so it must be okay."

"But…"

"There're no buts, Helen. Why are you making such a fuss? It's not even your jewel!"

"That's not the point!" Helen walked around the stand

"Ah ladies!" You're back." Albert boomed. "You wouldn't believe the number of visitors we've had in here this week. I can't remember the museum ever being so busy."

"It was very busy few years ago when the museum exhibited some rare Egyptian antiquities." Helen gestured around the room. "Of course back then everything was safely behind bullet proof glass."

"Bullet proof glass is a thing of the past." Albert shrugged. "You ladies ought to move with the times." He walked off before Helen could respond.

"That does it!" Helen was angry. "I'm going to prove the jewel can be stolen!"

"Keep your voice down!" Marion looked around nervously. "And just how do you propose to do that?"

Helen smiled. "Why! I'm going to steal it, of course."

"You're what!" Gina almost exploded. "You're not serious! We must get you out of here; the jewel is beginning to addle your brain."

Outside on the pavement, Marion spoke sharply to her friend. "For goodness sake, stop all this nonsense!" But then her curiosity got the better of her. "How do you plan to steal it?"

Helen shrugged. "I have an idea – but I'd need your help."

"No!" Gina shrieked. "Count me out!"

"Me too!" Marion sounded adamant.

"At least listen to what I have to say. I'll treat you to a coffee while I explain."

In the café, Helen outlined her plan. "Together, I'm sure we could pull it off."

"But why should we want to?" wailed Gina.

"Because Albert sees us as three useless women who know nothing about security matters," said Helen, excitedly. "We could prove him wrong. Come on, where's your sense of adventure? Think of Indiana Jones; think of King Solomon's Mines, think of…"

Marion held up her hands. "Okay! We'll discuss it."

For the next few days, they talked of nothing else. "We'll give the stone back, once we've proved it could be stolen," Helen assured them.

"But if we're caught, will the police believe we were testing a theory?" said Marion thoughtfully.

"Well we must make sure we aren't caught!" replied Helen. Nevertheless Marion had a point. "Leave it to me."

On the appointed day Gina sounded unsure. "Are we ready for this? Perhaps…"

"Of course we're ready!" snapped Helen. "What about you, Marion? Do you want to back out too?"

"No." She swallowed hard. "I'm as ready as I'll ever be."

"Good!" Helen took a deep breath. "Now remember, Albert must be in the room when we do this. It would be even better if another member of the public was there too."

At the museum, Albert was already standing by the jewel when Helen and Marion strode into the room. As arranged, Gina loitered in the corridor waiting for the signal.

"Hello, Albert." Helen glanced around the room. Another man was examining a painting – perfect.

"Ah! You're back again, ladies." Albert leapt to attention. "It seems you can't stay away from our exhibit."

Taking a deep breath Helen curled her fingers around the handkerchief in her pocket before nodding at Marion. They were on!

The ladies moved closer to Albert. "What can you tell us about the stone?" Marion asked.

Helen took Marion's arm. After making sure the man was still looking at the painting, she fixed her eyes on the stone. "The jewel seems to hold a fascination for us," she said loudly.

"Good! Good!" Albert swaggered. "It was found a long time ago… What the…" he yelled, as the room was thrust into darkness.

"Albert! What's happened?" Helen grabbed at him. "I can't see!"

"Help us, Albert." Marion tugged his arm.

Just then the emergency power swung into action and as Albert had predicted, everything happened at once.

"Get off me, woman!" Loosening Helen from his arm, he glanced around the room.

"Oh my goodness we're trapped!" wailed Marion, looking at the shutters. "Get us out of here."

Albert wasn't listening; he was staring at the stand. "The jewel has gone!" Horrified, his voice rang out above the sirens.

"Gone! Are you sure?" said Helen.

"Of course I'm sure, you stupid woman! Look for yourself."

"But how can that be? The cage is in place, yet there's no one trapped in there."

"I can see that!" Albert bellowed. "It's your fault. If you hadn't held me back, I'd have caught the thief." His eyes fell upon the man across the room. "Stay where you are!" he roared.

"It's not my fault." Helen was indignant. "We were both afraid when the lights…"

"Shut up, woman!" Albert yelled, striding towards the man. "I'm Chief of Security. Empty your pockets!"

The man emptied his pockets onto the floor. "I haven't got your jewel," he spluttered.

"Albert!" cried Marion. "Open the shutters! We want to go home."

"No one is going anywhere until the police get here!"

Once the police arrived, Albert pointed to the man. "He's the thief."

"Leave it to us now; you escort the women outside," ordered the inspector.

Reluctantly, Albert led Helen and Marion to the front door. Gina was already outside.

"Would you call a cab please?" asked Helen. "I feel faint with all this excitement."

A crowd had gathered outside and the museum administrator was talking to them.

"I'll handle this." Stepping out onto the pavement, Albert took over. "Go home everyone. The excitement's over. I've apprehended the thief. It would take a very clever fellow to transport the jewel out of the museum. Not even I, Chief of Security, could do that."

"You didn't catch the thief!" exclaimed the administrator. "These three ladies took the jewel."

Albert stared at them in disbelief.

"Yes," said Helen. "And very easy it was too, especially as you carried it out of the building for us." She pointed to his jacket. "It's in your pocket."

"How?" he spluttered. Pulling the stone from his pocket, his hands turned purple.

"Simple!" said Helen, triumphantly. "I tried to tell you that your cage was set too close to the stand. It's so easy to reach over and snatch the jewel without stepping over the rim. The gap between the electricity going off and the emergency power coming on allowed me to do just that. Once I had the stone, Marion helped me slip it into your pocket. Gina supplied the power cut via the mains box in the corridor, which, I might add, wasn't locked! A real thief could have retrieved the stone from your pocket once you were all out of the room. Once I explained my concerns, your administrator was keen to let us try."

"Show me your hands!" Albert uttered.

Helen's hands were clean. Reaching into her pocket, she pulled out a deep purple handkerchief.

"You kindly informed us of the purple solution so I dyed this and used it to grab the stone. Even if you had checked me out, I'd have got clean away." She glanced at the others and grinned. "It appears, Albert, your system couldn't trap a thief after all."

Dear reader,

We hope you enjoyed reading *A Surprise For Christine.* Please take a moment to leave a review in Amazon, even if it's a short one. Your opinion is important to us.

Discover more books by Eileen Thornton at https://www.nextchapter.pub/authors/eileen-thornton-mystery-romance-author

Want to know when one of our books is free or discounted for Kindle? Join the newsletter at http://eepurl.com/bqqB3H

Best regards,
Eileen Thornton and the Next Chapter Team

About the Author

Eileen Thornton lives with her husband Phil, in the pretty town of Kelso in The Scottish Borders
Website: www.eileenthornton.com
Blog: http://www.lifeshard-winehelps.blogspot.com/
http://www.twitter.com/eileenmaud2

Novels by Eileen Thornton

The Trojan Project - http://bookShow.me/B00KGSAD7Q
Divorcees.Biz - http://bookShow.me/B00F3KD6JY
Only Twelve Days - http://bookshow.me/B00G6ZN7WG

You might also like:

Cupidity by Lucinda Lamont

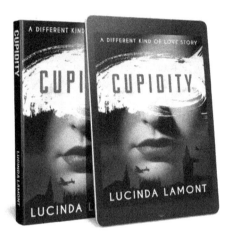

To read first chapter for free, head to:
https://www.nextchapter.pub/books/cupidity